BODYGUARD BEAR

BODYGUARD BEAR

PROTECTION, INC.
1

ZOE CHANT

AUTHOR'S NOTE

This book stands alone. However, it's the first in a series about an all-shifter private security agency, Protection, Inc. If you'd like to read the next books after you finish this one, *Defender Dragon (Protection, Inc. # 2)*, *Protector Panther (Protection, Inc. # 3)*, and *Warrior Wolf (Protection, Inc. # 4)* are available now.

TABLE OF CONTENTS

CHAPTER ONE

Ellie

Ellie McNeil was not having the best night of her life.

It was 3:49 AM, and she felt every second of the sleep she hadn't gotten. Her eyes burned, her feet hurt, her head throbbed, and her muscles ached with weariness.

Remind me why I volunteered for the overnight shift, again? Ellie asked herself. *Oh, right. Because I really, really need the money.*

And also, she had to admit, because sometimes there was nothing more exciting than being the paramedic on call in the middle of the night.

This wasn't one of those times.

Ellie and her partner, Catalina Mendez, had taken call after call since their shift had begun at midnight, speeding out in the ambulance with sirens screaming. And not a single call had been for an actual emergency. In between calls, Ellie and Catalina debated over which was more ridiculous, the drunken frat boy who thought his sleeping roommate was dead because he'd stopped snoring or the elderly man who thought he had a fever because he'd forgotten to turn off his electric blanket.

As the ambulance sped through increasingly sketchy neighborhoods, Ellie decided that it wouldn't hurt to close her eyes. Just for a second…

Catalina brought the ambulance to a stop with a screech of brakes, nearly flinging Ellie into the dashboard.

"Wakey, wakey!" Catalina sang out, her voice bright with sadistic cheer. She was a night owl by nature, and volunteered for overnight shifts because she actually preferred them.

"I was *not* asleep," Ellie retorted. "I was just… resting my eyes."

"That's what sleep *is*," Catalina pointed out. "Up and at 'em, Ellie. Just two more hours till we can go home and cuddle up with… Uh, cuddle up."

Ellie repressed a sigh as she grabbed her medical bag. At 6:00 AM, Catalina got to go home and cuddle up with her cats. Ellie had nothing to cuddle with but her pillow.

One year, eight months, and two weeks since I last had sex, Ellie thought glumly. Not that she was counting.

It could easily be another year— or two, or five, or ten— till she found a man willing to put up with a woman who spent half her nights saving lives away from home. Catalina made do with short-term flings, but Ellie didn't want to settle for anything less than a committed relationship. Which meant that she'd settled on nothing at all.

When Ellie scrambled out of the ambulance, the icy night air chilled her lungs and face, shocking her to full awareness. She forgot about her weariness and lack of romantic prospects, and focused on her job.

"Review call," she said automatically.

Equally automatically, Catalina recited, "Male, age eighteen, awoke disoriented and combative. Call placed by mother."

"Bet you a pizza he snuck out and partied too hard," Ellie suggested.

Catalina elbowed her in the ribs. "I'm not taking your sucker bets."

The apartment building faced an alley too narrow for the ambulance to park in. They left the ambulance parked on the wider street that the alley intersected, and walked down the dark, garbage-strewn alley toward the apartment belonging to the disoriented, combative male and his mom.

Ellie's smile vanished as they hurried up the stairs. She and Catalina might privately joke about their jobs— they had to have a sense of humor, or they'd lose their minds— but once they were in the presence of their patients, the paramedics were completely focused on doing the best they could for them. Even if the boy was just drunk or high, Ellie and Catalina would examine him, make sure he was all right, and reassure his worried mother.

The woman who opened the door was tiny and white-haired, ninety if she was a day. "Oh, thank God you're here! My poor baby Ricky!"

Ellie frowned in confusion as she followed the woman, who seemed way too old to have an eighteen-year-old son. Maybe the 911 operator had misheard 'grandmother' as 'mother.'

The woman pointed dramatically. "Here he is!"

Ellie bit down on her lower lip to stop herself from bursting out laughing.

Ricky was a fat, fluffy, contented-looking Angora cat. He blinked up and yawned at them from his perch on the back of the sofa.

"Ricky is a cat," Catalina said, her voice quivering slightly.

"He's my baby," the woman corrected them. "I woke up and went to get a drink of water, and I reached out to pet him as I passed by. He always purrs when I pet him, but tonight he meowed and twitched his head like he was going to bite me. My poor baby!"

"I think you just startled him," Ellie said soothingly.

The woman shot her a doubtful look. "I guess that could be it. He does look better now, don't you, baby? But better safe than sorry! Aren't you going to examine him, just to be sure?"

Fighting to keep a straight face, Ellie said, "Catalina, why don't you do the exam? I'll just go out and radio the hospital with our estimated time of return."

As Ellie walked past her partner, Catalina whispered, "You owe me a pizza."

"Come on, you love cats," Ellie whispered back, and made her escape.

Once she was safely out the door, she gave in to laughter. Poor baby Ricky, the world's most pampered cat!

Ellie was still smiling as she walked down the stairs. It was calls like these that reminded her of why she loved being a paramedic, despite the crazy hours and the lonely nights at home. Whatever else you could say about the job, it was never boring.

She entered the alley. Blinking down the dark strip of asphalt, lined with garbage cans and buildings with darkened windows, Ellie tried to remember which end of the alley led to the street where they'd left the ambulance. One dented trash can looked vaguely familiar. Yawning, she turned right.

The alley stretched on for longer than she remembered walking when they'd first come to the apartment. The only light was from distant street lights, and everything was dim and shadowy. The still air smelled strongly of mold, oil, and rotting garbage. There was no sound but the occasional rumble of a car driving by several streets away.

Uneasy, Ellie wondered if she'd gone the wrong way. Then she came to a dead end at a brick wall. It was a T-shaped intersection, with even darker and narrower alleys leading to the left and right.

Definitely the wrong way, she thought. She turned around to go back.

"Are you sure he's dead?" The voice came from the alley to her left. The speaker was a man with a low voice.

Ellie froze in her tracks. Obviously, someone was in desperate need of medical help. Normally she'd have run forward to offer her assistance. But the speaker's tone chilled her blood. She felt certain that he *wanted* someone to be dead.

"I'm pretty sure, Mr. Nagle," said a different man, sounding slightly nervous. "I shot him three times."

Ellie knew that the best thing for her to do was to walk away quietly and call the police. But she hadn't become a paramedic because she liked to play it safe. She stepped behind a dumpster, careful to place her feet away from anything that might snap or squish or crunch. Her heart pounding, she cautiously peered out into the alley. Though the light was dim, her eyes had adjusted to it. She could see perfectly.

Two men stood in the alley, looking down at the limp body of a third man. One man was in his fifties, tall and gray-haired, dressed in a black suit that looked out of place in the filthy surroundings. The other was in his late twenties, a big bruiser in jeans and a blood-spattered T-shirt, holding a gun. But it was the sight of the man down on the ground that made Ellie stifle a gasp.

She wasn't shocked because he was bleeding, or because he might be dead. Ellie had cared for lots of injured people, and seen her share of dead-on-arrival bodies. What shocked her was that she recognized the man.

She didn't know him personally, but she was familiar with his face. She'd voted for him at the last election, barely three months ago. It was Bill Whitfield, the new district attorney of Santa Martina. He'd run on the promise to fight organized crime.

He was dead. She'd been a paramedic long enough to know that, even from a distance. There was nothing she could do for him.

"Shoot him again," the tall man ordered. "In the head. Execution-style. Just to send a message."

"Okay, Mr. Nagle," the younger man— the hit man— replied.

He adjusted his aim, then shot the dead man in the head. The gun must have been silenced; it made a soft popping sound, not a loud bang.

Ellie flinched. Her heart was beating so hard, she felt like it would smash through her ribs. She had to get out of there and call the police, before these men saw her and killed her too. She took one last look, memorizing their faces, then turned to tip-toe away.

A rat emerged from beneath the dumpster and scurried over her foot. She jerked backward, barely managing to stop herself from letting out a yelp. But the rat was as surprised as she was. It bolted madly into a nearby heap of beer bottles and soda cans, producing a tremendous clatter.

"What's that?" demanded Mr. Nagle.

"Someone's there!" the hit man shouted.

Ellie flung herself forward, a second before she heard another soft pop. The bullet barely missed her head, hitting the brick wall beside her. Chips and dust exploded out, and a sharp pain stung her cheek.

She ran like she'd never run in her life. Sheer terror lent her speed. She heard the men shouting behind her, and heard another soft pop. Her lungs burned as she forced herself to go faster, expecting any second to feel the impact of a bullet in her back. Or to feel a brief explosion of pain in her head, and then nothing ever again.

She burst out of the alley, looked around wildly, and spotted the ambulance. Ellie yanked out her keys, dove for the rear door, wrenched it open, and scrambled into the rear compartment. She heard another soft pop as she slammed the heavy metal door. Ellie flinched, but she felt no pain. She hadn't been hit.

Then she scrambled forward and slammed her hand into the button that turned on the lights and siren. Bright lights flashed, and the siren screamed.

She hoped that would be enough to scare the murderers away, but she had one more way to make sure. Ellie hit the button that projected her voice outside of the ambulance like a bullhorn. Usually she and Catalina used it to order careless drivers to get out of their way.

"GET AWAY FROM THE AMBULANCE." Ellie's voice boomed out, amplified and deepened. "I'VE HIT THE EMERGENCY ALERT. THE SWAT TEAM IS ON ITS WAY."

There was no emergency alert, unfortunately. But she bet the murderers didn't know that.

Black spots suddenly danced before her eyes, and she felt her knees give way. She sank down to the floor, dazedly thinking, *So this is what it feels like to be so scared that you pass out.*

Then she remembered that when she saw patients on the verge of collapsing from shock, she told them to put their head between their knees. Ellie put her head between her knees. Slowly, her vision cleared, though she still felt shaky. She fumbled for the radio button, and finally got it turned on.

"Ellie McNeil here," she said. "Paramedic on duty at Ambulance Forty-Nine. I've just witnessed a murder."

Ellie sucked down the dregs of her fifth cup of black coffee and glanced at her watch. 1:00 PM. If she'd had a normal night at work, she'd be at home now, fast asleep. If she was a normal person with a normal job, she'd be eating lunch.

Instead, she'd spent the last eight hours at a police station, telling and re-telling her story to multiple sets of detectives, and identifying photos of the men she'd seen. Whoever the murderers were, the police knew about them; the hit man had his photo in one of the books of mug shots, and Mr. Nagle had appeared in an envelope of photos a detective had shown her.

Ellie yawned again, wishing the police had allowed Catalina to stay and keep her company. Catalina had offered, but the police had sent her home. Now Ellie was exhausted *and* bored. The cops had given her coffee and sandwiches, but she'd been awake for twenty-four hours now, with no sign of being allowed to leave. And they'd been crappy sandwiches and worse coffee.

Worst of all, the last cop who'd spoken to her, Detective Kramer, had confiscated her purse to "take it into evidence." Then she'd been left alone in the room without even her cell phone to distract her.

To her relief, Detective Kramer returned with her purse and handed it back to her. "Sorry about that. Just procedure."

Ellie gratefully took it. "Thanks. Can I go home now? You've got my number— you can call me whenever you arrest those guys, and I can come in and ID them."

Detective Kramer rolled his eyes. "Sure you will."

Ellie stared at him, baffled. "Why wouldn't I?"

The detective gave her a startled look, then slowly whistled. "I thought you were putting me on. But you really have no idea who Mr. Nagle is, do you?"

Frustrated, Ellie snapped, "No! Now will you please tell me what's going on?"

Detective Kramer sat down across from her. "Have you ever seen a movie called *The Godfather*? Nah, you're probably too young…"

"Of course I've seen it."

"Nice to know people still watch the classics," the detective remarked. "Well, Wallace Nagle is the Godfather. He's the head of organized crime in Santa Martina. No one testifies against him, because—"

"They'd wake up with a horse head in their bed," Ellie said. She'd thought the night couldn't get any worse, but her stomach lurched at the thought.

Detective Kramer raised his eyebrows. "They wouldn't wake up at all. As you saw. Now, I can offer you Witness Protection…"

Ellie had heard of that. "You mean, I change my name, leave Santa Martina, move to some tiny town no one's ever heard of, get a different job, and never have any contact with any of my friends or family for the rest of my life?"

"That's right."

"No way," Ellie said. Imagine never seeing her brother again! Or Catalina. "Absolutely not. Who'd do that?"

"No one." With a sigh, the detective stood up. "Well, thank you for your time. I'm sure you'd testify if you could. You can go home now."

He turned and headed for the door.

Ellie jumped up, raising her voice to halt him. "Wait a second. I never said I wouldn't testify. I just won't go into Witness Protection."

Detective Kramer froze, then slowly turned to face her. "Let me make sure I heard you right. You're not willing to do Witness Protection, but you *are* willing to testify against Wallace Nagle."

"That's right."

"And you realize that he's going to try to kill you. And that he can. Easily. I appreciate your courage, Ms. McNeil, but unless you go into Witness Protection, you won't live to testify."

The detective's words made Ellie's entire body tingle with anxiety. But she'd seen an innocent man ruthlessly murdered. How could she *not* testify, no matter how dangerous it was?

But she wasn't willing to give up her entire life, either. How could she agree to abandon her family and friends, and never see or speak to any of them again? She didn't want to give up her job— she loved being a paramedic in the big city. And on the off-chance that she found a man who loved *her*, job and all, how could she have a real relationship when she could never even tell him her real name?

On the other hand, she'd never have a relationship with anyone if she was shot by one of Mr. Nagle's hit men.

Ellie bit her lip, trying to think of alternatives to ruining her life, ending her life, or letting a vicious murderer get away with it. Catalina wasn't just her partner, she was Ellie's best friend. But good as she was at emergency medicine and pedal-to-the-metal driving, she couldn't fight off a hit man. Ellie's brother Ethan was completely capable of protecting her, but he was on some secret Marine mission. He wouldn't be able to leave it even if she had any way of contacting him, which she didn't.

"Can't the police protect me?" Ellie asked. "You want to put Nagle away, right? Then keep me alive so I can do it."

"We don't have a budget for round-the-clock protection," Detective Kramer replied.

At that point, Ellie's stress hit maximum. She wasn't hot-tempered normally, but hearing that the cops couldn't afford to save her life made anger burn through her body. "I bet your boss could find some money for getting rid of the Godfather! If you can't help me, I want to talk to the watch commander."

"That won't be necessary," Detective Kramer began.

"I want to talk to the watch commander," Ellie repeated.

"He's busy."

She folded her arms across her chest. "Fine. He can see me when he's ready. But I'm not leaving till I've talked to him."

The detective seemed taken aback. "Hold on. I'll see what I can do."

He hurried out. The door shut behind him, leaving Ellie alone and feeling like she'd just made the worst mistake of her life. She couldn't bring herself to deny what she'd seen, but the idea of being hunted like an animal made her heart start pounding again.

I'll be safe. The watch commander will find the money, and then I'll have a police officer to protect me, she told herself.

The thought didn't make her feel much better. Detective Kramer might be good at solving crimes, but he looked like he spent more time eating donuts than chasing down criminals. And while the detectives she'd spoken to had been nice, several of the patrol officers had openly ogled her curves when she'd walked through the station.

With the luck Ellie was having that night, she'd probably get Officer Creeper, one step up from a mall cop. He'd stare at her generous breasts and big ass, get in her way as she tried to work, lurk creepily in his car outside her apartment at night, and shed a trail of donut crumbs wherever he went. He'd breathe heavily and stand way too close to her. And if anyone attacked her, he'd be so out of shape that *she'd* have to protect *him*.

Worst night of my life, Ellie thought.

CHAPTER TWO
Hal

Hal Brennan was exercising alone in the gym of Protection, Inc., when he got the call.

Stinging sweat dripped into his eyes, and even his powerful muscles felt the burn as he lifted the bench press bar high. But one of the advantages of owning your own private security company was having your own private gym. He and the other shifters on his team could lift weights heavier than any human could manage without having to worry that some outsider would see them and contact the Guinness Book of World Records.

Weight-lifting wasn't his favorite form of exercise. That honor went to hiking in the woods, preferably as a grizzly bear. But as far as gym-based exercise went, lifting was the best. Living in a city— hell, being human— was so damn complicated. It made him appreciate things that were simple. And lifting was as simple as it got. No rules to tie him down. Just Hal vs. the iron. It was as close as he could get while human to feeling like a bear, with a bear's straightforward desires.

The shrill tone of his cell phone broke his concentration. It was his private phone, with a number he gave out only to a select few. Which meant that the call was from his parents, or from one of his team, or an emergency. Whatever it was, he couldn't ignore it.

Hal replaced the bar on its rest and reached down from the bench to pluck his phone from his gym bag. He glanced at the screen. Yep. Parents.

"Hi, Dad," Hal said. "How's it going?"

His father's deep, gravelly voice, which everyone said sounded just like Hal's, rumbled out from the phone. "How's your search for a mate going?"

Hal grimaced. "It's not."

"Why not?" Dad demanded, as if they hadn't had this conversation a hundred times already. "Get out there and look for her! Your mother wants grand-cubs."

"You mean, *you* want grand-cubs."

Unruffled, Dad replied, "The entire clan wants grand-cubs."

There was a scuffling noise, and then he heard his mother's voice. "It makes us so sad to think of you all alone in the big city." She gave a melodramatic sigh. "Aaaaall aloooooooone."

Hal was torn between the desire to laugh and the urge to throw the phone across the room. "I'm hardly alone. I have my team. You know how close we all are. We're like brothers and sisters."

As if she hadn't even heard him, Mom repeated, "Aaaaall aloooooooone. The city is no place for a bear. It's full of violence and loud noises and electric things. Bears need a peaceful, quiet life, fishing and eating honey and sleeping in the sun. Drop this silly city thing and come back to the woods."

"Mom," Hal said, trying to keep a grip on his patience. "Dad. We've had this talk. I'm not like you. I need excitement. I need danger. I need to make a difference to people. And I'm not going to find any of that in the woods. There is absolutely nothing in the forest that can threaten a bear."

"Who wants to be threatened?" Dad asked.

At the same time, Mom exclaimed, "I want cute, furry grand-cubs to love and spoil! Go find a mate and settle down!"

"Mom…" Hal sighed. "I don't *want* a mate. And I don't want to settle down. I like my life exactly the way it is. I do my own thing, and no one tells me what to do. My job is dangerous and unpredictable. I have to run off to deal with emergencies on a moment's notice. No woman is going to want a man who lives like that. And I don't want to make some nice woman miserable trying to change me into something I'm not."

"You'll think differently once you actually meet your mate," said

Dad. "You'll be willing to make any sacrifice."

"You *need* a mate," Mom said earnestly.

"I don't need anyone," Hal argued, frustrated. "I can handle anything the world can throw at me. By myself!"

"All bears need a mate," Dad replied.

Hal gave up. "I have to get back to work. Talk to you later!"

He hung up, then settled back down on the bench, returning the cell phone to the bag. Hal loved his parents and his clan, but he'd lose his mind if he had to live with them. The forest was great for a vacation, but he wasn't made for a peaceful life, and he had absolutely no desire to settle down.

My mate, he thought, unable to help himself. *I wonder what she's like? I don't need her, but does she need me? Am I screwing up her life by not looking for her?*

He hoped not. With any luck, she'd find someone else she could be happy with.

An unexpected pang of loneliness stabbed right through his heart at the thought of his mate with another man, followed by a surge of possessiveness.

No one but us gets our mate, Hal's bear growled.

"I don't need anyone!" Hal's voice rang out, startling himself. He hadn't meant to speak aloud.

He took a deep breath, trying to regain the sense of peace he'd felt when he'd been lifting. Eventually it returned, washing over him like a cool shower.

He'd just reached for the bar to do another set when his phone rang *again.*

"Goddammit," he muttered to himself, then picked it up. This time it was his main police contact in Santa Martina, Watch Commander Carl Gutierrez.

"Brennan," Hal said. "What's the emergency?"

Hal listened to the watch commander's story with growing amazement. "She's going to testify against *Nagle?* Seriously?"

"She is. And that's not all," Gutierrez said grimly. "She's refused to go into Witness Protection. So I need your help. I've found a grant to pay for her to be protected around the clock. I want the best person you have."

Hal opened his mouth to say that he didn't hire anyone who wouldn't be the best person at any other security company, and anyone on his team could protect the witness. Instead, he heard himself saying, "I'll guard her myself."

He headed to the locker room to shower, wondering all the while why he felt so compelled to take on the assignment. He rarely did straightforward bodyguard work. Maybe he was drawn to the challenge of protecting someone Nagle was gunning for.

As he was getting dressed, two of his team members came in. Of all his team, Nick and Lucas probably had the least in common, which was why Hal had assigned them to work together. He'd hoped it would break the ice.

Nick entered first, slamming the door open like he wanted to knock some sense into it.

"Hold the door." Lucas's hard-to-place accent made even those simple words sound like a line from some very classy play.

"Don't fucking order me around." Nick gave the door a shove back, apparently hoping to slam it in Lucas's face.

A hand adorned with several gold rings caught the door, then gave it a matching shove that threatened to knock it off the hinges.

If Hal didn't move fast, ice wouldn't be the only thing that got broken. He cleared his throat.

Nick whipped around to look at him. His surprise was briefly replaced with a "who're you looking at" challenge that Hal hadn't seen directed at him in a while. Then the challenge vanished. It had been a long time since Nick had been the alpha of a criminal werewolf pack, fighting ferociously to maintain his power.

"Hey, Hal." Nick stripped off his shirt and armored vest, then tossed them aside, exposing a muscular torso covered in an elaborate tattoo of wolves hunting deer in a deep, dark forest. They were shifter tats, so they were less obviously criminal than if he'd belonged to a human gang. But Hal knew what they meant. One drop of blood on a deer for each fight won, one drop of blood on a wolf for each fight lost, and one dead deer for each kill.

"Hi, Nick," Hal said.

Lucas strolled in, radiating unconcern. "Good day, Hal."

"Hi, Lucas."

Lucas removed his shirt and bullet-proof vest, then set them neatly down on the bench. His angular chest was marked by an intricate pattern, glittering gold. It looked like a tattoo, but Hal knew that he'd been born with it.

Hal made sure he was looking at both of them as he asked, "How's the job going?"

"Fine," Nick said shortly.

"It goes well," Lucas replied.

Hal stared at them until they both dropped their gaze. He didn't believe in micro-managing his team, but he also didn't believe in letting problems simmer till they exploded.

"Is there an actual problem, or do you two just wish you had a different partner?" Hal inquired.

The men glanced at each other, Nick's green eyes meeting Lucas's golden ones, and seemed to come to a truce.

"No problem," said Nick. "Guess I'm just used to working with someone I can have a beer with after work."

"There is no problem. I am not used to working with..." Lucas paused just long enough to make it sound like he was about to say something stunningly insulting, then concluded, "...others."

Hal addressed both of them as he said, "Well, get used to it. I'm about to take a bodyguard assignment myself, so I won't be around to babysit."

As he'd intended, the men stopped shooting pissed-off glances at each other, and turned their pissed-off glances on Hal.

"Yeah, whatever, man," Nick said. "We're cool."

"Babysitting is not required," Lucas replied icily.

They went into the gym together, leaving Hal alone. He caught a snatch of their conversation just before the door closed. It didn't sound friendly, but at least it didn't sound hostile. It seemed like his ploy had worked.

Lucas was his newest hire, and it was always hard to join a team that had already bonded with each other. Hal had assembled his team one by one, so everyone on it had been the new guy once. But even on a team of shifters, Lucas stood out. He was a dragon shifter. Hal hadn't even known they existed until he'd met Lucas.

Hal set aside thoughts of his team as he left the locker room and went to the parking garage. He had his own job to focus on now.

As he drove to the police station, he couldn't stop wondering about his new client, Ellie McNeil. What sort of woman was brave or crazy enough to agree to testify against *Wallace Nagle*, Santa Martina's answer to the Godfather? That man practically ruled the city.

Hal would have understood it if Ellie had been a criminal herself, desperate to cut a deal to escape prison. But according to Gutierrez, she was an ordinary citizen— a working woman, a paramedic on the late shift. She must be terrified. She was probably regretting her decision already.

He pulled into the police parking lot and went into the station, half-convinced that he'd find that she had changed her mind about testifying and gone home.

Watch Commander Gutierrez indicated a room. "She's in there."

Mildly surprised, Hal headed for the door. He had to duck his head to go in. Most places weren't built for men his size.

Ellie McNeil sat with an empty paper coffee cup in her lap, her head lowered, her hair hanging forward to hide her face. She seemed to have dozed off in her chair. Everything about her posture spoke of utter exhaustion, which didn't surprise him. She'd worked all night, then witnessed a murder and nearly gotten killed herself, and then had been questioned at a police station for eight hours. Talk about a rough night!

He couldn't see her face behind a tumble of curling dark blonde hair. It was a pretty color; it reminded him of clover honey. Her practical paramedic uniform didn't conceal her generous curves. Though her shirt and pants were cut loosely, Hal could see the shape of her wide hips, her plump thighs, and her lush breasts. She had exactly the sort of body he liked: big and soft and curvy.

With thinner women, Hal always worried he'd hurt them by accident. They seemed so fragile, especially given how big and strong he was. Besides, he didn't like how bony they felt. But with a woman like Ellie, big and voluptuous, he wouldn't have to worry about anything but whether she was enjoying herself as much as he was. Besides, he liked the way curvy women felt. He imagined running his hands over the gentle swell of her belly, the delicious weight of her breasts, the silky softness of her thighs…

Hal forced himself to stop that train of thought. He'd come to protect her, not to hit on her. The fact that she was incredibly hot was completely irrelevant. Unfortunately.

He cleared his throat. "Excuse me."

"Wha—" Ellie jumped, her head jerking up. So she *had* been dozing.

Hal stepped forward, holding out his hand. "Hi. I'm Hal Brennan, your bodyguard."

She pushed her hair out of her face and looked up. Their eyes met.

The force of the contact nearly knocked Hal backwards. It was an earthshaking, heart-stopping jolt of recognition.

Mine!

The roar of Hal's bear was so loud that he half-expected Ellie to have heard it. But of course, she hadn't. She just sat there, her head tilted quizzically, her kissable pink lips parted in a smothered yawn.

Everything about her was perfect, from her snub nose to her ocean-blue eyes to the sprinkling of freckles on her upper arms. He knew nothing about her other than that she was a paramedic and beautiful and sexy and incredibly brave, but he loved her already.

Holy shit, Hal thought. *She's my mate.*

He was nearly overwhelmed with joy. There was the other half of his heart and soul, sitting right there in front of him. If he took a single step forward, he could sweep her into his arms, kiss her and caress her, and never let her go. They'd be together forever.

If Nagle didn't kill her first.

Hal was jerked from happiness to a protective fury in the blink of an eye. He'd finally found his mate, and the most powerful crime lord in the city was trying to murder her.

He knew then that he'd give his life to protect her.

"Mr. Brennan?" Ellie asked. "Are you feeling all right?"

Hal was jerked back into reality. Ellie was peering at him, looking concerned. God knew what sort of weird impression he'd just made on her.

"Yeah," Hal said shortly. He couldn't think of anything but getting her away from Nagle, immediately. "Come on, let's go."

"Oh, good." She stood up, then swayed wearily.

Hal caught her elbow, steadying her. Her arm was warm and soft in his hand. "Easy. I know you're tired. You can sleep in my car."

Ellie straightened, rubbing her eyes. "I'm not *that* tired. My apartment is only about ten minutes from the station."

Hal shook his head as he began to lead her to the door. "We're not going to your apartment. You have to get out of the city."

She stopped abruptly, pulling her arm out of his grasp. "I'm not leaving the city. Didn't Watch Commander Gutierrez explain that to you? He said he was assigning me someone to protect me here, in Santa Martina."

Hal turned to look her in the eyes, trying to convey how serious he was. "First of all, I'm not a police officer. I'm private security."

She looked dismayed rather than relieved at that. "You're a *security guard?*"

"I'm not a mall cop," Hal replied. "I run an elite private security company. We provide bodyguards for politicians and celebrities— and private citizens like you. Nobody's ever been hurt under our protection."

"Oh. Well, great. Then you can protect me right here."

"No!" Hal exclaimed. "I have to get you out of the city!"

Ellie's blue eyes narrowed, reminding him that she was one tough woman. "Mr. Brennan, can you protect me or not?"

Hal gritted his teeth. Of course he could protect her— he'd showed up expecting to guard her right there in Santa Martina. But that was before he'd known that she was his mate. His instincts, not to mention his bear, were roaring at him to not merely stand between her and any possible threat, but to get her far away from anyone who might try to harm her.

"Because if you can't," she went on, "I'll talk to the watch commander again and ask him to assign a police officer."

"I can protect you," Hal said immediately. "But you'd be a lot safer if you left Santa Martina."

"I already had this conversation," Ellie replied. "I'm not going anywhere. I already ran through my sick leave this year. If I take off for more than a couple days, I lose my job. Anyway, I thought no one ever got hurt under your protection."

Take her home and keep her safe, Hal's bear demanded. *Grab her and carry her away to the forest!*

I can't do that, Hal replied. *But I will take her home. To* my *home.*

"All right," Hal told her. "I'll guard you here. But you can't go straight to your apartment. I need to have my team check it first."

"Check it for what?"

"Hit men. Bombs."

"Oh." The delicate skin of her throat bobbed as she swallowed. He could see the fear under her cool exterior, and it made him want to kill the men who had frightened her.

He laid his hand on her shoulder. Touching her, even through cloth, gave him a surge of desire. It was hard to do nothing but keep his palm there, comforting and still, when he wanted to scoop her into his arms, kiss her, and hold her safe and tight.

But she'd shown no sign of responding to him the way he had to her. She wasn't a shifter— she knew nothing of mates. He had to give her time to get to know him. In the meantime, he'd be professional.

"I swear, I'll keep you safe," Hal said, willing her to believe it.

Ellie let out a sigh and leaned into his hand, as if she liked having it there. Then, to his disappointment, she pulled away. "So, do we go to a hotel?"

"No. We're going to my place. I have a guest bedroom."

"Why not a hotel? Security, again?"

Because I want to welcome you into my home, Hal thought. *Because it'll make* me *feel safe knowing that you're in my lair, where I can protect you.*

Fishing for a reason that would make sense to her, he said, "Yeah, security. And..." His gaze fell on the empty coffee cup. "It's got a cappuccino machine."

For the first time, Ellie smiled. It was like the first bright burst of sunlight on a cloudy day. Sure, it was at the promise of coffee rather than at him, but he'd take it. "Cappuccino, huh? Lead on."

CHAPTER THREE
Ellie

Ellie was so exhausted that she dozed off in the passenger seat of Hal's car. She woke up while he was still driving, and looked in confusion at the rain-streaked windshield and the city streets. Why was she in a car? Where was she? And who was that man in the driver's seat beside her?

Then memory returned in a rush. Fluffy baby Ricky. The murder. Her entire life turned upside down. Hal Brennan, the hot bodyguard.

She stole a glance at Hal. He drove steadily, not seeming to notice that she was awake. His ruggedly handsome face was intent on the streets, his hazel eyes seeming to take in everything. She was sure that he was scanning for danger, alert but cool.

She relaxed in her seat. Hal seemed like the kind of guy who could handle anything— the opposite of the creepy mall cop she'd imagined. It wasn't just that he was something like six foot five of solid muscle. She'd met lots of big guys who were useless in a crisis. It was his attitude. He radiated competence and courage.

He also radiated heat. Literally. They sat close enough that she could feel his body heat against her side, comforting... and arousing.

Ellie stifled a sigh, telling herself, *You are not going to sleep with the hot bodyguard.*

He was a professional, and she was his job. There was nothing more between them than that, and no matter how close he stuck to her side until she could testify, there never would be. She could look, but not touch.

With that in mind, she took a good long look. Her first impression of Hal had been a sleepy, startled blur of *tall* and *burly* and *whoa, gorgeous eyes.* But now that she was slightly more rested, she had time to savor the details.

He was big all over, built like a football player or weightlifter, but perfectly proportioned. He had none of the overly chiseled, vein-bulging grotesqueness of a 'roid rage bodybuilder; his impressive musculature looked like he'd gotten it the hard way, from regular exercise and a physical job. She especially like the swelling muscles of his shoulders and forearms, covered in smooth tanned skin.

His features were masculine, good-looking and a little rough-edged. Strong jaw. Broad nose. He would have looked hard and intimidating, except for the cute cleft in his chin and the soft depths of his eyes. His eyes… she could look at his eyes for hours. They were hazel, half-way between green and brown, framed by long eyelashes. In the bright lights of the police station, they had looked green as summer leaves; walking to the car under dim parking lot lights, they had seemed mahogany brown.

Hal glanced at her, catching her looking. A hot blush rose up beneath her skin, making her face burn from ear to ear.

"We're almost there," he said.

"No one followed the car?" She was half-joking, torn between fear and feeling like she was in some action movie she could turn off if she got bored with it.

Hal replied as seriously as if that had been a completely reasonable question. "No. Believe me, I'd notice."

I bet you would, she thought.

He pulled up before an underground parking lot, punched in a code to open the gate, drove in, and parked. Ellie was so tired that she had barely registered that they had arrived before Hal had walked around, opened her door, and offered her his hand.

She knew he was only doing it because she was visibly exhausted, but it felt like the sort of sweetly old-fashioned gesture an especially gentlemanly man might make on a first date. No one had opened a car door for her in years.

Ellie gratefully took his hand, trying to hide her smile. Maybe she'd pretend she was on a date with Hal. It felt better than facing the reality that he was only there because the most powerful criminal in the city wanted her dead.

Hal's hand closed over hers. It was huge and warm, completely enveloping hers. He easily lifted her to her feet. She swayed. Her feet had fallen asleep, and her legs felt like jelly. He caught her around the waist, supporting her.

"Sorry," Ellie muttered, embarrassed. She tried to stand straight, but she couldn't bring herself to pull away from him. His solid strength was so comforting.

"You've got nothing to apologize for," Hal said. "You worked all night, you witnessed a murder, you got shot at, you had to run for your life, and then you spent the next eight hours being interrogated in a police station. Anyone would be a little shaky after that."

"You wouldn't."

"Sure I would," Hal replied as he led her to an elevator. "When I got through SERE training, I was so exhausted, I slept for three days straight. That's Survival, Evasion—"

"Resistance and Escape," Ellie finished, then grinned at his startled look. "My brother Ethan is a Recon Marine. But he wouldn't tell me anything about SERE training, except that they teach you to resist torture and live off the land. He said he ate a bug at one point, but I'm not sure if that was part of the wilderness survival or part of the torture."

Hal laughed. "Wilderness survival. Probably. Where's your brother now?"

"I don't know. Somewhere classified. I guess it's just as well. It would drive him crazy knowing that I'm in danger and he can't protect me. Hopefully it'll all be over by the time we can get in touch."

They got into the elevator. Instead of buttons, it had a code pad. Hal punched in another code, and the doors slid shut.

"You weren't kidding when you said your building was secure," Ellie remarked.

"Yeah. It's completely safe. You can stay as long as you like, you know. You could stay till the trial's over."

It was a ridiculously generous offer. "I can't just invade your home for who knows how long— months, maybe!"

"Sure you can." Hal's intense gaze dropped, and he actually shuffled his feet. For the first time since she had met him, he seemed awkward and uncertain of himself. "I mean— it would be more convenient for me, if you lived with me instead of me living with you. Since we're going to be joined at the hip anyway."

The elevator stopped. Ellie started to step forward as the door slid open, but Hal put out a hand to stop her, scanning the corridor until, she supposed, he was satisfied that there were no lurking hit men.

"Okay, clear." He led her to his door.

As he punched in yet another code to open his apartment, the reality of the situation sank in for Ellie. He was going to be living at her house! For months, probably. His guys were probably inspecting her home right now. She wished she'd made the bed and washed the dirty dishes from last night's dinner. Her face heated again as she realized that she couldn't go in alone and clean it up before Hal saw it.

Not to mention that *she* didn't have a spare room. Where would Hal sleep? Her sofa was more like a loveseat. He was way too tall to stretch out on it. But they could hardly share the bed.

A wash of heat surged through her at the thought of them doing exactly that. She could just imagine cuddling up next to Hal's naked body. It would be even better than cuddling up against him clothed, like she was practically doing right now.

Hal opened the door for her and led her inside. "Home sweet home."

She looked around the apartment. After all the security and coded touchpads, she'd expected something sterile and sleek, filled with high-tech gadgets and hard, uncomfortable furniture, with the homiest touch consisting of a rack of guns. Instead, it really did radiate home sweet home.

The brown leather sofa and armchairs were worn and softened by use, and the moss-colored carpet was soft and thick beneath her feet. The brown-and-green color scheme made the apartment seem like it was part of a forest. A cozy forest. Bookcases filled with beat-up paperbacks lined the walls, along with pictures of people and huge trees. There was no television.

Hal apparently hadn't been expecting visitors either. The counters of the open kitchen were cluttered, there were books piled on the sofa, and a pair of boots lay in the middle of the floor. But the lack of spick-and-span neatness only made his apartment seem lived-in and welcoming. If it had been perfectly tidy, Ellie would have been afraid to sit down in case she wrinkled the sofa.

"Sorry about the mess." Hal hastily kicked the boots under the sofa.

"Don't worry about it," Ellie replied. "Now I'm less embarrassed about you seeing the mess at my place."

"I'm sure it's not that bad. Anyway, I don't have a leg to stand on." He made a grab for the books on the sofa, but Ellie got to them first. She was curious about what he liked to read.

The first one was about what she'd have expected, a Dick Francis thriller called *Odds Against*. It didn't surprise her a bit that Hal would like reading about tough guys fighting against the odds.

The second one, *Code Name Verity*, was also unsurprising at first glance: a historical adventure about a British spy captured by Nazis. Then Ellie read more of the back cover. She could hear the surprise in her own voice as she read aloud, "'An exciting and moving tale of female power and female friendship?'"

Hal's eyebrows lifted. "What, you think I wouldn't read a great adventure story just because it's about women?"

"Lots of men wouldn't," Ellie pointed out.

The same men who don't give me or Catalina half the respect they'd give a male paramedic, she thought. *The same men who would never date a woman with a dangerous job.*

"I'm not lots of men," replied Hal.

His tone conveyed more meaning than his simple words, as if he'd read her mind: *I'm not one of those assholes.*

Is he... flirting? Ellie wondered. Then, with some disappointment, she concluded, *Can't be. He must just mean he's not a sexist pig.*

Which is also good, she hastily told herself. *It would be awful having to be with him constantly if he didn't respect me and I didn't like him.*

To distract herself from the sad reality that Hal would never flirt with her, she looked through the other books he'd left scattered on the sofa. *Homicide Special*, nonfiction about Los Angeles homicide detectives. *Three Parts Dead*, a fantasy novel about a sorcerer hired to resurrect a dead God. *Cash: The Autobiography*, by Johnny Cash.

"Is this what you do instead of watching TV?" Ellie passed the stack to him. "Or is it in the bedroom?"

Hal put the books back on the shelves. "No. I grew up in the country. My family was kind of... back to nature. We didn't have a TV, so I never really got in the habit. What about you? Are you a book person or a TV person?"

"I'm about 50-50." Examining his bookcases, she added, "We like some of the same books, though. I'm really into mysteries and thrillers. Especially romantic suspense. Gunfights and kissing, my favorite things."

"Mine too," remarked Hal.

Flirting? Ellie thought again. *I… think so?*

But lots of people were just flirtatious in general. It didn't mean they were flirting specifically with the person they were with, or that they had any intention of doing anything about it.

Trying to figure it out made her tired. She couldn't suppress a jaw-cracking yawn.

"You must be exhausted," Hal said. "And I know the food at the police station sucks. What did they give you, burned coffee and a processed cheese sandwich?"

"Processed cheese, wilted lettuce, and mystery meat. And a bag of chips."

"They've gotten better, then. They didn't used to provide chips."

Ellie laughed. Despite the weirdness of her bodyguard taking her to his own house, which couldn't possibly be standard procedure, she felt more relaxed now that she was there. "I really like your place. It's so cozy."

Hal stopped arranging the books and turned toward her. "I'm glad. I want you to feel at home here. Now, would you rather go straight to bed, or would you rather have something to eat first?"

"It's a tough decision, but if I don't eat first, I'll wake up starving in the middle of the night."

"Then have a seat. I'll make you something." He indicated the sofa, then headed into the open kitchen.

She couldn't help noticing how well he filled out his pants as he walked away from her. Since he had his back to her, she took the opportunity to enjoy the sight of his ass and legs, not to mention his broad shoulders and huge biceps.

Look, but don't touch, she reminded herself.

If there was one thing that could make her life even more horrendous than it already was, it would be having sex with her bodyguard, followed by the inevitable messy break-up, followed by being joined at the hip to her new ex-boyfriend for God knows how long. Just the thought of that made her tired. More tired.

She sank down on the sofa. It was as soft as it looked, inviting her to lean back her head and nap. She had to force herself to keep her eyes open. At least she had something entertaining as a distraction.

"Is there anything you don't like?" Hal called. "Mushrooms? Bacon?"

"I love mushrooms and bacon," she called back.

Watching Hal cook, she realized that his kitchen was messy because he actually used it. He chopped vegetables with terrifying speed and a very large knife, grabbed spice jars from a rack without consulting a cookbook, and flipped the contents of a frying pan without spilling a single bit of whatever it was he was cooking. Ellie's stomach rumbled embarrassingly as the smells of frying eggs, potatoes, and bacon filled the room.

She was impressed that he could cook, and more impressed that he was willing to cook for a client. That couldn't possibly be part of the job description. Well, she'd enjoy it as a "Welcome to Witnessing" gift. Her own cooking was limited to taking off the plastic wrapper before she stuck something frozen in the microwave.

She must have dozed off for a moment, because the next thing she knew, Hal was setting a tray table in front of her.

"Oh—" Ellie looked at the feast laid out in front of her. He'd made her an omelet, country-style potatoes, bacon, and a glass of orange juice. "This is exactly what I'd have ordered if I'd gone to a restaurant. How did you know?"

He settled down beside her with his own tray table full of breakfast-for-lunch, the same as hers with the addition of a mug of coffee. "It's what I'd have wanted if I'd gone through what you did. Comfort food."

Ellie dug in. As soon as she tasted the food, she was as impressed with his cooking skills as she was with his thoughtfulness. The potatoes were crunchy on the outside and soft on the inside, the bacon was at the exact sweet spot between crispy and chewy, the omelet was stuffed with melted cheese and mushrooms, and the orange juice was fresh squeezed.

"Where'd you learn to cook like this?" she asked.

"Like I said, I grew up in the country. My whole family cooks. We hunt, too." He hesitated briefly before he went on, "We'd shoot a deer and break it down, and make our own venison chops and steaks and sausage."

"Sounds fun," Ellie replied. "My brother Ethan likes to hunt."

"Do you ever go with him?"

She should have been prepared for the question— after all, she was the one who'd mentioned Ethan— but a wave of sadness caught her off-guard.

He must have caught her expression, because he said, "Did I say something wrong?"

"No." She could have brushed off the question or changed the subject, but something about Hal, his sweetness or his solid strength, made her want to tell him. They'd only ever have a professional relationship, but even so, she wanted him to get to know her better.

"Ethan and I are twins," Ellie said. "We're fraternal, of course, but we looked a lot alike when we were little. And our personalities are similar, too. You don't know me well enough to know what that means, but—"

"I think I do," Hal said. "Let's see. You're both brave. Risk-takers. Daredevils. You both want to do what's right. And you'll both make sacrifices to do it."

She stared at him. "What are you, some kind of bodyguard mind-reader?"

He shrugged. "He's a Recon Marine who ate a bug in SERE training. You're a paramedic who's going to be the first person ever with the nerve to testify against the man who scares the entire city shitless. It's obvious."

Maybe it was, but Ellie wasn't used to having men call her brave. And she was even less used to hearing them call her a risk-taker as if it was a good thing.

Awkwardly, she went on, "Well, Ethan and I were really close when we were young. Then our parents got divorced when we were ten. It was awful. They both accused each other of cheating, and they got in a custody battle. The judge awarded me to Mom and Ethan to Dad. They were both so pissed off that they moved to opposite ends of the country. Ethan and I got to see each other maybe once a year. We promised to move to the same city once we were old enough to make our own decisions. And we did. But he joined the Marines, so we still only see each other about once a year."

Ellie blinked back tears, then snatched up a napkin and scrubbed at her eyes. She hated crying, and she especially hated crying in front of other people. It made her feel weak. "Sorry. I don't usually get all emotional like this. It's because I'm so tired."

Hal put his hand on her shoulder. "Don't worry about. It's been a rough day."

His touch brought her comfort. Maybe even enough to be worth having him see her cry. But she at least didn't want to *keep* crying. Hastily, she said, "What's your family like?"

"Oh, they're great," Hal said cheerfully. "Very outdoorsy. Dad's a carpenter, and Mom makes fancy jellies and jerky and so forth. They live in this little town north of here, with a bunch of my other relatives, and they all like to get together and go hunting and hiking and fishing and picnicking and—"

As Hal went on describing how loving and cozy his family was, Ellie couldn't help comparing it to hers, with her parents who hated each other, her bitter mother, the father she barely knew, and the brother she loved and hardly saw.

And this *is why none of my relationships ever work out,* Ellie thought. *It's not just my schedule. It's because once I tell guys about my background, they decide I'm too damaged to have a relationship. Maybe they're right. Why would a guy like Hal ever want to be with a woman like me?*

Hal broke off abruptly. "I'm sorry. I'm being a complete asshole."

"What?" She was bewildered. "What are you talking about?"

"All that stuff about how great my family is." He let out a long breath. For the first time, she saw his usual calm break into anger. "I mean, everything I said is true. It's just not the whole truth. They *are* nice. They also want a lot of stuff from me that I've never been able to give, and they've pressured me to be someone I'm not for my entire life."

"Who do they want you to be?" Ellie asked, barely stopping herself from blurting out, *"But you're perfect."*

"A small-town man leading a small-town life. They want me to live quietly in a cabin with a wife and a bunch of kids, and never use a gun for anything but hunting. Ellie, I was a kid like you and Ethan, and my entire family lost their shit every time I took a risk or broke a rule. I couldn't stand it. I ran away when I was seventeen and enlisted in the

Navy." He squeezed her shoulder. "So don't feel like you're the only one with the messed-up family. Join the club."

She was surprised and touched by his story… and that he'd confide her. "Do they still get on your case now?"

Hal nodded, then gave a wry smile. "My parents were on the phone this morning, telling me to move to the country and have lots of babies."

"Do you even have a girlfriend?" Ellie spoke without thinking, then instantly blushed. "Sorry. That's none of my business."

Hal's hazel eyes focused on hers, and she forgot her embarrassment as she gazed into them. Their rich brown-green reminded her of a forest. All those colors. She could get lost in them. "No. No girlfriend."

In the silence that fell, she became acutely sensitive to how close together they were sitting. His hand was still on her shoulder. All he'd need to do to kiss her was lower his head a little. She could imagine the press of his warm lips against hers, imagine the scratchiness of his stubble.

He stood up abruptly. "I know you're tired. I'll show you the spare bedroom."

She stood as well, irritated at herself for her own imaginings. Just because Hal didn't have a girlfriend didn't mean he was into her. He was just a sweet, considerate, sexy guy who would make some future girlfriend deliriously happy.

Some future girlfriend who wasn't her. That future girlfriend had all the luck. Ellie hated her already.

Oblivious to her ill-wishes against his non-existent girlfriend, Hal showed her the bathroom, and gave her a spare toothbrush and one of his own shirts to sleep in. She brushed her teeth and took a shower, then put on Hal's shirt. Ellie was a big woman, but it fell to her knees.

It was a black-and-red checked flannel shirt, buttoned down the front. She rubbed the hem between her fingers. It was soft, well-worn, and though it was clean, it had a very faint, lingering scent that she knew had to belong to Hal. Wearing it made her feel cozy yet lonely, as if she was both close to Hal and reminded of how far away he really was.

When she got out of the bathroom, he said, "If your apartment isn't safe to return to by the time you wake up, I'll have my team pack up some of your clothes and bring them. Now get some rest."

"Do I get a cappuccino in the morning?" she asked playfully.

"Absolutely," he promised. "I'll even make a fancy pattern on the top with chocolate shavings, how's that sound?"

"Sounds like something to look forward to. Good night—" Ellie realized that it was still barely afternoon. "I mean—"

Hal smiled. "Good night, Ellie."

"Good night, Hal."

Ellie closed the door of the guest bedroom and flopped down on the bed, too tired at first to even turn off the light. She lay on her back and looked around the room. Like the rest of Hal's apartment, it was cozy. The mattress was firm but not too firm, the pillows soft but not too soft.

This bed is too big, she thought with a grin. *This bed is too small.*

As she reached out and clicked off the light, her last thought before she sank into a dreamless sleep was, *But this bed is juuuust right...*

Ellie lay helpless in an alley. She tried to get up, but her limbs wouldn't move. She couldn't feel the ground beneath her back.

Paralysis, *she thought.* Nerve damage. Spinal injury.

Nagle stood over her, looking down with eyes as cold as a winter frost. "You can still back out. Promise not to testify, and I'll let you live."

Terrified, she tried to agree. Part of her hated herself for her own cowardice, but another part was desperate to live. But her lips wouldn't open. No matter how hard she tried, she couldn't speak.

Nagle snapped his fingers at the hit man. "Kill her. Oh, and kill her bodyguard, too."

She couldn't turn her head, but she could move her eyes to follow Nagle's gesture. To her horror, she saw Hal sprawled beside her. He'd been shot. Blood drenched his shirt and jeans. He was lying in a pool of it, shiny and black under the harsh white streetlights. His eyes were closed.

But he was still alive. She could hear his breathing, fast and shallow. His skin was sweaty and pale beneath the tan.

Hypovolemic shock, *Ellie thought.* Apply direct pressure to stop the bleeding, stabilize cervical spine, give oxygen, start an IV, and transport immediately.

She struggled to get up, to get to him, to throw herself across his body to protect him. But she couldn't move.

His eyes fluttered open. "Ellie? Help me…"

She couldn't move.

Hal was going to die, and she couldn't help him.

It was all her fault.

Her fault.

Her fault…

Ellie sat bolt upright in bed, gasping, her heart pounding. It was pitch black. She didn't know where she was.

Hal is dying—!

Then she felt the firm but not too firm mattress beneath her, and remembered.

It was just a dream, she told herself.

But her heart kept on slamming against her ribcage like it was trying to break out. She couldn't get that picture out of her head, of Hal lying there in a pool of blood. She'd treated enough people for gunshot wounds that her treacherous imagination had made every detail absolutely realistic.

The memory of the dream was so vivid, Ellie could practically hear his pained breathing. If she hadn't been paralyzed, she could have reached out and touched his face. She knew what his skin would feel like, clammy with shock and slippery from sweat.

Her vision adjusted to the dark, allowing her to see the dim rectangle of the door. She swung her feet over the side of the bed, determined to see for herself that Hal was all right. It was the middle of the night, so he was probably asleep. The apartment was silent. But she knew she'd never be able to get back to sleep without checking on him.

She'd just peek into his bedroom— *like a creepy stalker,* the sane part of her mind informed her— and listen till she heard him breathing. Then she'd go back to bed. Once she got the idea, she couldn't wait to carry it out. She dashed forward, her bare feet silent on the plush carpet, and threw the door open.

It slammed into something solid. She stared at the shape of a huge man lying on the floor, then realized that it was Hal. He let out a grunt of pain as he sprang to his feet, far more quickly than she'd ever seen a man of his size move.

"Ellie!" Hal exclaimed. She could only see him in silhouette, but his tall form bent toward her, every line of his body expressing concern. "Are you all right?"

"Sorry," Ellie said. "I'm fine. Are *you* all right?"

Hal gave a rumbling chuckle. "I'm fine. Are you sure you are?"

"Yes!" She was too embarrassed to say, *I had a nightmare.* Or, worse, *I dreamed that you were dying, and it was the worst nightmare I've ever had.*

She'd only just met him. It made no sense for her to feel so attached to him, or to feel such tremendous relief to see him alive and well. And it would be hugely awkward if she let him see how she felt, when all she was to him was a job.

He flicked on the light switch and stepped aside so she could pass him. She blinked in the bright light, rubbed her eyes, and started to walk past him. Then she stopped and looked back.

Hal stood barefoot on the hallway's hardwood floor, fully dressed and holding a gun. His brown hair was tousled into a bedhead that made her long to smooth it back. He'd obviously been asleep…

…but not in bed. She'd slammed the door into him because he'd been lying on the floor.

She was unable to completely believe her own memory. "Were you sleeping on the floor here?"

Hal ducked his head. "Um…"

"*Why?*"

"I'm your bodyguard."

"Yeah, but…" Ellie looked again at the hardwood floor. "Not even a pillow?"

"Well…"

"Is that normal procedure? Sleeping on the floor outside your client's bedroom, fully dressed with a gun in your hand?"

A pink flush crept along Hal's cheekbones. "No."

The lingering fear and horror of her nightmare faded, replaced by curiosity, even amusement. Hal looked so deeply embarrassed. And there was something simultaneously hilarious and adorable about an enormous tough guy like him blushing. "Then why were you doing it?"

He squared his shoulders as if he was about to charge some terrifying enemy. Then, unexpectedly, he replied, "Let's make a deal. I'll tell you why I was sleeping on the floor if you tell me why you bolted out of the room like that."

She hesitated. "You go first."

Hal's steadfast hazel gaze never left her face as he said, "I know my home is secure. But I couldn't relax. I kept imagining someone hurting you. So I got my gun and stood outside your room. But then I realized that if I was sleep-deprived, I'd be damaging my own ability to protect you tomorrow. So I lay down on the floor with my back against the door, to make sure that anyone who tried to get to you would have to go through me first."

Ellie was both touched and amazed. "Do you always do that?"

"Never. Just for you. Ellie, you're... You're special." He fell silent, gazing deep into her eyes. His right hand clenched over the pistol grip, and he pulled his left forearm against his chest, as if he was stopping himself to doing something with it.

You're special.

Her heart began to pound as hard as it had when she'd woken up from her nightmare, but with excitement and arousal rather than fear. She knew that Hal was standing like that, all his muscles tense, because he was holding himself back.

And she knew what he was holding himself back from. All the uncertainty of the night before vanished like smoke in a wind. Ellie knew that Hal wanted to touch her as much as she wanted to touch him. But just as she knew that, she also knew that he wasn't sure she felt the same way.

"Want to know why I opened the door?" She couldn't quite catch her breath. Her voice wavered.

"Yes." Hal's voice came out in a low growl that sent a bolt of desire straight to her heart. And also lower down.

"I dreamed that you'd been shot." Her voice was shaking again. "You were dying. You asked me to help you, but I couldn't."

"Oh, Ellie." Hal replaced his gun in his holster, then enfolded her in his strong arms, pulling her tight into his body. She leaned against him, listening to the thud of his heartbeat. She could feel his body heat, and hear every breath he took. "It was just a dream. I'm fine. *I* protect *you*. Don't worry about me."

"I know it was a dream," Ellie muttered into his shoulder. "But it felt so real. I had to see for myself that you were all right. I was going to sneak into your bedroom and listen to you breathe, like a creepy stalker."

Hal burst out laughing. At first she was hotly embarrassed. Then his deep, infectious laughter made her realize how absurd she'd sounded, and she laughed as well.

"You can stalk me any time," Hal said.

She took a deep breath and looked into his eyes. "Even into your bedroom?"

"Especially into my bedroom."

Look, but don't touch, Ellie's cautious side warned her. But she and Hal were already touching.

Too late, she thought.

As if he had read her mind, he said, "If you want to say no, say no."

"I'm saying yes." Ellie tilted her head back, presenting her lips for a kiss.

Her entire body seemed to melt from the heat of his mouth. Dizzy, she clung to him, molding her softness against his hard solidity. He stroked her shoulders, her back, her sides as they kissed. She slipped her hands under his shirt, exploring the angles of his bone, the firmness of his muscle, the silky smoothness of his skin.

This close, she could smell his masculine scent, and it made her feel wild and desperate. She kissed harder and wriggled against him, as if she could merge her body with his. She felt the huge, hard rod of his erection, and she rubbed herself against it, drawing a rumbling groan from him. She loved knowing how much she could affect him, and rubbed against him again. A bolt of desire went through her at the friction. He gasped, and so did she.

With another groan that was almost a growl, Hal snatched her up into his arms. Ellie yelped, startled.

"Hey, it's okay," Hal said. "Do you want me to put you down?"

"No, I was just surprised." She reclined in his arms, letting her head fall back against his shoulder. "No one's ever lifted me before. I thought I was too heavy."

"You're not too heavy," Hal replied, striding toward his bedroom. "Or too light." He bent to kiss her. "You're just..." Another kiss. "Exactly..." And another. "Right!"

She giggled, remembering her sleepy thoughts about the too big/too small/just right bed.

He kicked open the door and took her into his bedroom. To her total lack of surprise, it had more bookcases, plus a teetering stack on the bedside table. There was no light that she could see, but the room was filled with a dim white glow, like moonlight.

Then she looked up. There was a huge skylight, showing the night sky and a three-quarters moon. The bedroom *was* lit by moonlight.

"I love the skylight," Ellie said.

"So do I," Hal said. "It makes me feel almost like I'm out in the woods. We could make love there for real some day."

Ellie tried to conceal her surprise. It wasn't at "make love" instead of "have sex." She'd guessed before that Hal was an old-school romantic. It was at the "some day." He was already thinking of this as a relationship, not as an ill-advised one-night stand. Ellie didn't know whether to be delighted or unnerved. How heartbroken was he going to be if this relationship lasted all of one week?

How heartbroken was *she* going to be?

Then he laid her down on his enormous bed and kissed her, and she tipped over into delight. She wanted to kiss him forever. Or at least as long as she could. Even one week would be better than one night.

Even one night would be better than never.

It was impossible— they'd only known each other for one night— but a feeling swelled up in Ellie's heart at the touch of his lips, a feeling hot and warm, passionate and tender, possessive and protective.

She couldn't call it anything but love.

It was crazy. But it was true.

Oh, well, she thought. *Hal called it: I'm a risk-taker.*

I hope he is too.

He straightened up, took off his holster, and put it on the bedside table. Then he stripped off his clothes and stood naked in the moonlight. Ellie lay back and relished the sight of him. As impressive as he was clothed, he was magnificent in the nude.

His rock-hard erection was the biggest she'd ever seen, but it was perfectly proportioned to his height and burly build. He looked like some heroic statue made to larger-than-life scale. She let her gaze travel over his perfectly sculpted six-pack, the elegant hollows over his pelvis, and his heavily muscled shoulders and chest.

His tousled hair and eyes looked black in the moonlight. But despite the lack of color, she could easily read his expression. He was looking at her not only with lust, but with tenderness. Maybe even with love.

She might be a risk-taker, but she didn't dare to ask.

Instead, she said, "You look great. You should be naked all the time."

Hal let out a rumbling laugh. "I want to see you naked now. Fair's fair."

She loved how eager he sounded. It was flattering… and a huge turn on.

"Go ahead," she said. "Take off my shirt."

She expected him to pull it off, but instead he bent down and began undoing the tiny buttons, one by one. His huge fingers worked with surprising delicacy, brushing against her uncovered skin as each button came free. Ellie didn't know if he was doing it like that to tease her or himself, but she lay there and positively *ached* with desire.

Finally, the shirt was off, and her own nude body was exposed to his view. His gaze traveled over it, so hungry that she could almost feel it on her skin. She loved seeing him look at her. It made her feel like the most beautiful and sexy woman in the world.

"You're so gorgeous," he said. "You have the most incredible body I've ever seen. I can't believe I didn't just rip that shirt off you!"

Ellie grinned, but her amusement melted into desire as he knelt over her. She could feel the heat coming off his body, and smell his personal scent. She reached up and tangled her fingers in his silky hair.

He kissed his way down her body, licking and nibbling and caressing. Her nipples hardened as he stroked his tongue around them, wringing moan after moan from her throat. Her hands clenched over the swelling muscles of his shoulders as the ecstasy of his touch grew to incredible heights. Everywhere he touched or licked felt aflame with pleasure, as if he'd left trails of heat in his wake.

"God," Ellie murmured. "The things you do to me—!"

She felt his breath warm against her skin, felt his lips move against the tender skin of her belly as he replied, "You ain't seen nothing yet."

She could hardly imagine. But she was obviously in good hands. "Bring it on."

He moved lower. She moaned in anticipation, knowing that soon she'd feel his mouth on her slick folds. Then he was licking at her, sending incredible waves of pleasure through her body. She could sense how much he enjoyed tasting her, now licking at her sensitive clit and at her folds, now moving to kiss her inner thighs, now using the tips of his fingers as well as his tongue.

Her hands gripped convulsively at the blankets as her pleasure built and built, sending her to the brink of orgasm. She couldn't even tell exactly what he was doing, but only knew that he was giving her an ecstasy like nothing she'd ever felt before.

"Hal," she gasped. "Hal—!"

She heard herself cry out wordlessly as she came, the sound pulled from her throat with the force of her orgasm. Then she was shaking with the aftershocks, each pulse a delicious pleasure, like a string of firecrackers after the first big burst.

Ellie lay relaxed and happy for what felt like a long time. Then she shifted, trying to snuggle closer to Hal's warmth, and felt the steel-hard rod of his erection against her thigh.

"Oh, no," she murmured. "I haven't done anything for you…"

Hal's voice vibrated through her body, soft and low as a purr. "Yes, you have. Just touching your body… Getting to taste you… Inhaling your scent… Feeling you respond to everything I did… Feeling you come… Ellie, I loved every second of it. It was a gift."

"Oh." The sincerity in his words touched her. No man had ever been so nakedly, honestly enraptured with her before. But he also sounded so utterly serious that she couldn't resist teasing him a little. "So you're good with just going to sleep now?"

Hal snorted and gave her ass a light smack. "I didn't say *that*."

Before she could say that she'd just been teasing, he added, "But if you're too tired, we don't have to do anything else. I could just… go into the bathroom and take care of myself."

Fascinated, Ellie kept silent, wondering how far he'd go with that. She was used to pushy men who thought of their own pleasure first, and hers a distant second. Would Hal really be fine with finishing up alone in the bathroom?

"Or…" he went on, sounding more hopeful. "I could take care of myself here. If you're not literally falling asleep, you could watch. That might be hot."

She burst out laughing. "I was kidding you, Hal. I'm not *that* tired. But if you'd rather do it yourself and have me just watch…"

"No, no!" Hal said quickly.

"Because it sure sounded like you were into that idea," she went on mischievously. "What's that called? Exhibitionism? Kinky!"

With great dignity, Hal replied, "It would only be exhibitionism if I did it in public. If it's in my own bedroom, it's… I don't know…"

Ellie took pity on him. "Something hot we'll have to try some day."

As soon as she said it, she realized that she too was assuming there would be a "some day."

"Absolutely," Hal assured her. "And hey, if there's anything *you* want to try, just let me know. But for now, how about the most basic thing there is?"

"You in me?"

"You got it."

"Sounds great." She leaned on her elbow and watched as he rummaged in a drawer on the bedside table, then fished out a condom. "XXXL?"

"Like everything else I wear," Hal said with a grin, rolling it on.

Ellie reached out to help him smooth the sheath over his huge erection. It was rock-hard, but the bare skin that she touched was velvety.

He drew in a jerky breath at the touch of her fingers. "Ellie, you drive me wild. I've never felt anything like this before."

"Me neither."

Hal stroked her cheek. "I don't just mean the sex."

Ellie felt overwhelmed by his presence, the sheer size of him as he held himself over her, his warmth, the touch of his skin, but most of all, by what he'd just said.

"Me neither," she whispered.

He kissed her as he slowly eased into her. She gasped at the feeling of stretching, not painful but startling; he was by far the biggest man she'd ever been with. She clasped her arms around his back as he began to move inside her. His skin was slick with sweat, and her hands slipped over his back. *She* was slick, inside and out. He slid easily into her despite his size.

It felt good— better than good. It felt amazing. Ellie rarely came twice in one night. But she could feel a second orgasm building within her. Every thrust sent her closer and closer to the edge. Her muscles tensed as she waited for it, her entire being caught up in delicious anticipation. Ripples spread out from her core, pushing her farther and farther out into an ocean of bliss.

"Come on!" she gasped, barely knowing what she was saying. "Take me— Take me there—"

Hal was getting close too, his thrusts coming harder, faster, wilder.

"Yeah," Hal said, his voice a deep rumble. "I'll take you there— Whatever you need—"

His mouth came down on hers as he stroked in and out of her. One last hard thrust, and she felt his seed spill hot within her. Sparkling lights burst before her eyes, and her whole body exploded into shattering pleasure.

Then they were lying still, hot and sweaty, their limbs entangled. Hal stroked her face and kissed her lips, her throat, her cheek. She kissed him back, and pushed wet strands of hair out of his face.

Ellie stretched, relaxed and happy. Her whole body felt as if she was melting into a puddle. She cuddled up against Hal, and he held her tight.

"That was amazing," Ellie murmured.

"For me, too." Hal's low voice vibrated through her body. "*You're* amazing. I feel so lucky to have met you."

"Same here," Ellie replied. "Yesterday I thought I was having the worst day of my life. But now it feels like the best."

"I'm glad."

They kissed one last time, sleepy and sated and warm. His stubble scratched her chin. The musky scent of sex lay heavy in the air, lulling her like the world's greatest sedative. Clasped in Hal's strong arms, she fell into a deep and peaceful sleep.

CHAPTER FOUR
Ellie

Ellie woke with a delicious feeling of contentment. She stretched, touched warm skin, and jerked into a startled full awareness.

"It's okay." Hal's deep voice relaxed her instantly, as if it was a hypnotic cue.

He was lying beside her, his magnificent body stretched out nude atop the covers, unselfconscious and tempting. She searched his face for signs of regret, but found none. His expression held only tenderness and a sensual enjoyment of the sight of her own nakedness.

Look and *touch,* she thought.

"You're not sorry?" she asked.

"Absolutely not," Hal assured her. "And I hope you're not sorry, either. Last night was wonderful, and I bet it only gets better from here."

Her head spun with the thought of better sex than last night. "I'll hold you to it. But first... Do I remember you saying something about a cappuccino machine?"

He sat up. "At your service. Fancy coffee first, or shower first?"

"Shower," Ellie decided. "Want to take one together?" Then, considering his size, she added, "If we'd both fit..."

Hal laughed. "We will. I remodeled the bathroom when I moved in. It's roomy."

He leaned over and picked up his holster, looping it over one arm.

"You take your gun into the bathroom?" Ellie had almost forgotten the danger she was in, until that reminder.

"I take my gun everywhere, if I have a client."

Ellie was used to patients not telling her everything, so she caught the brief pause before he replied. "What about when you don't have a client?"

"Okay, you got me," he confessed. "I take it everywhere, period. It's a holdover from being a Navy SEAL. I like to know that I can always protect myself and others. I'd feel naked without it."

"I bet you could kick a lot of ass unarmed. Naked, even."

"I could." His tone wasn't bragging, but a simple statement of fact. "I'm not bulletproof, though."

Then, to her delight, he picked her up and carried her out. She nestled against his strong body, loving the skin-to-skin contact.

Inside the bathroom, he looped the holster over a hook, then set her down in the shower stall and stepped in with her. It was more than big enough for both of them.

She leaned her back against him, closed her eyes, and let the warm water wash over her. Ellie wasn't expecting anything more, but a woodsy scent arose, and she felt Hal's hands on her head. He shampooed her hair, massaging her scalp and working the suds into every bit of her hair. It was as intimate as it was luxurious. He held one hand over her forehead, to keep any stray trickles out of her eyes.

She sighed with pleasure when he was finally done, and tilted her head back to rinse her hair clean. "Thank you. Want me to do yours?"

Hal looked down at her. "I'm too tall."

"Thanks for not saying, 'You're too short,'" she replied. "Kneel down."

She had meant it only so she could do him the same sensual favor he had done her. But he knelt to her like a knight before a queen, going down on one knee to swear fealty and protection.

Ellie had seen a drawing of that in a book she'd read as a child. The image came back vividly to her mind as Hal knelt before her with his head lowered. Clear water cascaded over the powerful muscles of his shoulders and back.

The knight in the story had offered the queen his sword, saying, "My life for you." And the queen had sent him out to do battle on her behalf.

Ellie wondered just how far Hal would go to protect her.

She hoped she'd never have to find out. With any luck, his intimidating size and presence alone would scare off Nagle's goons.

Trying to push away thoughts of Nagle, Ellie busied herself shampooing Hal's hair. It was short but not military-short, thick enough for her to run her fingers through. It looked black when it was wet. She rubbed shampoo into it, massaging his scalp as he'd massaged hers. He gave a long sigh of dreamy pleasure, and leaned his head against her side.

When she finally moved the showerhead to rinse out the shampoo, Hal opened his hazel eyes and looked up at her. "You're the first woman who's ever done that for me."

She combed through his wet hair, enjoying its smooth caress between her fingers. "Those other women missed out."

Hal stood up, and they began to soap each other. Ellie couldn't decide which was sexier, running her soapy hands all over Hal's body, or feeling his huge yet gentle hands caressing her. Her nipples hardened and her breath quickened under his touch.

He bent to kiss her, and she felt his own hardness as she pressed up against him. The suds were slippery between their bodies, the running water a sensual tease. Hal put his hand between her thighs, stroking and teasing her slick folds. She could feel her own liquid heat running out and over his fingers. Her clit felt almost unbearably sensitive. Even the lightest stroke of his fingertips made her shudder with pleasure.

Her eyes shut, she reached out blindly and found his steely rod. She closed her fingers around it, and felt Hal's own shudder of excitement. His delicate skin slid over the rock-hard flesh beneath as she moved her hand up and down his shaft.

Heat pooled in her belly and sent out sparks throughout her body, each one setting its own little fire. She was trembling uncontrollably, caught up in the pleasure of his touch. He caressed her folds, her clit, and her inner walls, and she felt herself pulse around his fingers.

"I—" she heard herself stammer. "I'm almost— almost—"

She ground herself against his hand, rubbing herself against his soft skin, his hard bones. He pushed back, giving her a stronger touch. Her fists clenched and her muscles tensed, her entire body moving toward orgasm. Then she was over the edge, crying out with the strength of her climax.

For a long, lovely moment, she enjoyed the fluttering pulses of the aftershocks, each one a pleasure in its own right. Then Ellie returned her attention to Hal. Her eyes still closed, focused only on the senses other than sight, she stroked him steadily, listening to his breathing grow deeper and faster as she sent him to the brink.

"Ellie—" he gasped.

His seed jetted on to her belly, a splash of heat almost immediately washed away. She looked up at him, blinking through the water. Hal was leaning back against the wall, his head tipped back, his eyes closed. He looked so relaxed and happy.

He opened his eyes, and she knew from the tenderness in his smile that he was seeing her as she saw him, as something precious he'd been lucky to find. "You're so beautiful after you make love. Did you know that your cheeks turn pink?"

"They do?"

He nodded and kissed each one. "Like roses."

They dried each other off, and then Hal wrapped a towel around his waist. "Hang on. I'll get your clothes."

He took off, and returned fully clothed in black jeans, a blue shirt, and a heavy black overcoat. He carried a suitcase in one hand, and a bundle under his other arm.

He pushed the suitcase toward her. "Here you go. I had some of my team check out your apartment yesterday. Destiny packed your clothes. She figured you'd rather have a woman do it."

"Yeah." Ellie was glad to have her own clothes to wear, but she didn't like the thought of someone going through them, even if it was another woman. "So, I can go back to my apartment now?"

Hal shook his head. "Not yet. I'm putting in a security system, and it's still being installed. It'll take another day or so. Meanwhile, you need to wear this."

He held out the bundle. It was a heavy-looking black vest.

"Bullet-proof?" Ellie asked.

"Yeah. I'll show you how to wear it. First, put on a bra and a light tank top."

Ellie opened the suitcase, hoping Destiny had selected her nice bras rather than the ratty gym bras. To her relief, Destiny had thoughtfully packed several of each. Shoving the gym bras under a pair of jeans, Ellie took out a black lace bra and matching panties. The appreciation in Hal's expression as she put them on almost made up for having to prepare to get shot at. Then she put on a lightweight cotton tank top.

"It straps on like this." Hal settled the vest over her shoulders and showed her how to adjust it. It wasn't as heavy as she'd expected. "Now put something on top of it. Dress warm, it's a cold day."

The vest was invisible beneath the long-sleeved blouse she buttoned over it. Ellie put on black jeans and a red sweater, then asked, "Are you going to wear one, too?"

Hal opened his overcoat and pulled down the collar of the shirt beneath it, revealing his own armored vest. But before she could get too caught up in thoughts of people shooting at them, he said, "Let's have breakfast. I'll make cappuccino."

They went into the kitchen. The cappuccino was as good as promised, with a shaving of chocolate atop the foam, vaguely in the shape of a heart. Hal made scrambled eggs. Ellie, discovering that Hal owned a pleasing array of jams, managed to make toast without burning it. Much.

After breakfast, she said, "I need to call Catalina and tell her I'm okay. I'm sure she's wondering what's up."

"Wait." Hal walked across the room and fetched a disposable phone, which he gave to her. "Make your calls and texts from this. It's untraceable. And don't tell her or anyone where you are."

"Thanks." But her belly clenched at yet another reminder of how much danger she was in. It had even invaded something as normal as calling her partner and best friend.

She went to the guest bedroom and called Catalina, filling her in on as much as she felt was safe. Ellie didn't intend to tell her she'd had sex with Hal, and tried not to say anything at all about him other than that she was now protected by a bodyguard.

Catalina immediately said, "He's hot, right? Hunky hot bodyguard… and I mean BODYguard. If you know what I mean!"

"Nooooo," Ellie said unconvincingly.

Catalina pounced, certain via some sort of BFF telepathy. "He's already 'guarded' your body with his body, hasn't he? Ooh-la-la! You move fast! I hope it was good."

Ellie surrendered. "Yes, we did. Twice."

"Twice!" Catalina wasn't satisfied until Ellie gave her all the details. At the end, she asked hopefully, "Does he have hot friends? A hot brother? Hot bodyguard buddies?"

"No idea. But I could find out. And on a less sexy topic… Have you heard anything from our boss?"

"Oh, yeah, sorry," Catalina replied. "I meant to tell you right away. They're giving you a week's stress leave. So don't worry about that."

Ellie thanked her and returned to the living room, catching Hal while he was still on the phone.

"Yeah," he was saying. "So can you rustle up the rest of them? Thanks."

He shot her a slightly guilty glance as he hung up, and she knew he'd been talking about her.

"What now?" Ellie asked. "I can't go back to my apartment, and I'm not due back at work yet…"

"I'd like to take you to meet my team." Hal looked at her hopefully. He was obviously dying for her to agree.

"Is this like 'Come meet my family?'" She was touched that he'd want her to meet them.

"A bit. I'm closer to my team, in some ways. They're like me—" He stopped suddenly, making her wonder what he'd been about to say. Probably something involving classified jobs assisting the military.

She teasingly filled in his awkward pause. "Really great at oral sex?"

To her amusement and delight, the adorable pink flush again tinged Hal's cheeks. "God, don't put pictures like that in my mind. They're like my brothers and sisters. I was going to say, they're a bunch of adrenaline junkies."

"You know, I've never taken a boyfriend to meet my family. But I'd like to take you. My parents… Well, I told you how that is. But my brother's great. You should meet him. I think you'd really get along."

"I'd love to meet him when he comes home." Hal kissed her. "Come on. Let's go meet the family."

He took her down to the parking lot, as alert for trouble as he'd been when he'd brought her to his apartment, and drove her to a big office building. Then he escorted her through another series of touchpad-operated elevators and doors— she was definitely getting the sense that he knew what he was doing when it came to security— and into the headquarters of Protection, Inc.

It was a bit like she'd expected Hal's apartment to be: sleek and modern, full of high-tech gadgets and security cameras and furniture made of black leather and chrome. But it wasn't sterile or lifeless. There were human touches, like bowls of old-fashioned movie candy like junior mints and Jordan almonds, and pots of gorgeous purple orchids.

But what struck Ellie the most were the huge framed photos on the walls of wild animals in their natural habitats. She walked around the office, examining each one in turn. Each photo showcased a different animal: a huge grizzly bear slapping a salmon out of a river, a pride of magnificent lions lazing on the savannah, a tiger stalking a deer through a lush green jungle, a pack of gray wolves in a forest, a black panther lying on a tree branch with an unsettlingly predatory gaze in its yellow eyes, and a snow leopard caught in mid-leap from one icy crag to the next.

Then she got to the last one. It showed the sun setting over a European castle, with some winged creature— a hawk? A bat?— flying in the sky overhead. Ellie peered at it, then stopped and stared, and finally laughed. The flying creature was a dragon!

"I love watching people react to that one," an accented male voice remarked.

Ellie spun around, startled. A group of people were walking into the room.

One of the men offered his hand. "Hello. I'm Lucas. And the dragon is mine."

She glanced at him curiously as she shook his hand. Lucas was tall and slim, wearing an expensive-looking suit. She wasn't an expert on clothing, but she'd swear it had been tailored for him. He had gold and diamond rings on his fingers, and a gold chain around his throat. His features were sharp and chiseled, and his eyes were a brown so light that they appeared as glittering gold as his jewelry. Lucas didn't look like a man who'd do private security; he looked like a billionaire or a prince.

"Ellie McNeil," she said. "Pleased to meet you. Um… What do you mean, the dragon is yours?"

Hal explained, "When I hire a new team member, I ask them what animal… uh… represents them. You know, which one they're most like. Then I get them a photo of it, for inspiration. Lucas just had to make my life difficult."

Ellie laughed. "What a great idea! Which animals go with which people?"

"Guess," said another man. He offered her his hand. "I'm Rafael, but everyone calls me Rafa. I'm one of Hal's old buddies from his Navy SEAL days."

Rafa matched what Ellie had expected the entire team to look like: tall and muscular, though not quite as big as Hal. He had black hair as tousled as if he'd just rolled out of bed, smooth brown skin, and a charming smile. While Hal often seemed wary and guarded, constantly alert for any threat, Rafa seemed completely relaxed. Ellie could see at a glance that he was a ladies' man.

"Well? Which do you think is mine?" Rafa's tone was playful, but challenging, too.

This really is "Meet the Family," Ellie realized. *Rafa's playing "Are you smart enough for my best friend?"*

"Not a fair game, Rafa," Hal said, his voice dropping to a warning growl. "She only just met you. Maybe later…"

Ellie liked how Hal always tried to protect her, even from something as minor as being wrong in public. But she wasn't one to turn down a challenge. Especially when it involved making a good impression on people who were important to Hal.

She met Rafa's brown eyes squarely. "No, I'll guess now."

Hal's lips curved into the hint of a smile. She could see that he liked that she'd taken up the challenge and stood up to his buddy, whether or not she succeeded. "Watch out, Rafa. Ellie's coming for you."

She looked from Rafa to the photos. She already knew that Lucas was the dragon. Though she barely knew him, it felt right: the strangeness, the elegant power, the hoard of gold and diamonds. So what animal felt like Rafa?

The lazy sensuality, the physical power easily worn…

"You like going to bars and having women draped all over you, don't you? There you are." Ellie pointed to the photo of the lion, stretched out in the sun with his pride of lionesses.

Rafa winked at her. "Very good! Yes, I'm the king of beasts."

Two team members, a black woman as curvy as Ellie and a tatted-up guy who looked like a gangster, immediately pounced on Rafa, shoving him and making scornful noises.

"King of one-night stands," the curvy woman teased him.

48

The tatted guy gave him a hard but playful punch in the arm. "King of Vegas marriages!"

"No, come on," Rafa protested. "That was just that one time."

More scornful noises erupted, and Rafa and the tatted guy got into a scuffle. Ellie glanced at Hal, but he didn't blink an eye. Obviously, some roughhousing was normal in this crowd.

The black woman stepped aside, leaving the guys to it. She wore a cherry red tank top that showed off her cleavage and white shorts that showed off her ass, and looked like she'd just come from the gym. Like Ellie, she was curvy but strong, with muscle beneath the softness. Ellie liked her immediately, reminded of herself and Catalina, women making their way in the tough job they loved.

"I'm Destiny. And you don't have to play those macho games with me. I'm the tiger: fierce and *gorgeous*." Without even looking, Destiny shot out her fist and gave Rafa another smack on the arm. "Give her a break, Rafa! She's already squared off with the Godfather. She doesn't have to prove a thing."

The other woman, who had been standing back, added, "She's not auditioning for team psychologist. Hal vouches for her. That's enough for me." She stepped forward and offered Ellie her hand. "I'm Fiona. Pleased to meet you."

The two women on the team were a study in contrasts. Destiny was short and curvy, but Fiona was tall and slender. Destiny's skin was darker than Rafa's, her eyes a deep brown, and her hair tumbled to her shoulders in a mass of silky curls. Fiona's platinum blonde hair was braided, then pinned tightly into a bun. Destiny was cheerful and exuberant, Fiona cool and reserved. And unlike Destiny's ultra-casual attire, Fiona wore a business suit with flats that she could run in, and a loose jacket that Ellie guessed concealed an armored vest and a gun. Possible several guns.

"Thanks," Ellie said to both women. "I appreciate it. That being said… Fiona has got to be the snow leopard. Right?"

Fiona looked mildly impressed. "I am."

"Two for two," remarked the tatted guy, breaking off his scuffle with Rafa. He stuck out his hand. "Nick."

His smile didn't reach his eyes. Nick gave her hand a hard squeeze, gripping to the point of pain. Ellie suppressed a wince and squeezed back, pretending she was juicing a lemon. She looked right into Nick's eyes as she did so, thinking, *If the Godfather couldn't scare me off, you sure can't.*

Ellie wasn't anywhere near as strong as Nick, but he quickly let go. "Hey, no problem. Just checking."

"What the hell did you just do?" Hal demanded. Then he caught Ellie shaking out her fingers. "Want me to crush *his* hand for you?" Staring straight at Nick, he added, "I could do it."

She hastily stopped wringing her hand. Nick reminded her of Ethan when he'd been younger, all bad boy attitude and rebellion, backed up with real courage and grit. "No, we're cool. Right, Nick?"

Nick gave her a real smile this time. "We're cool."

Hal let out a long-suffering sigh, then snapped his fingers. "Shane. Don't be shy."

"Hello." The voice was a man's, quiet but attention-catching.

Ellie nearly jumped a foot in the air. She hadn't seen him before, nor could she figure out how he'd managed to get all the way across the room to lean against the wall beside her without her noticing.

Shane was almost as tall as Hal, but less burly. His muscle was lean, like a long-distance runner. His hair was cut short as a Marine's, covering his head like a plush black pelt, and his eyes were blue as the sea in winter. Like Hal, he seemed habitually watchful; unlike Hal, he didn't seem relaxed even in his own headquarters, surrounded by his teammates.

"Pleased to meet you." Shane held out his hand.

He didn't challenge her, glare at her, or try to crush her hand. His expression showed nothing but politeness. His hand was warm, his grip firm but no more than that.

There was absolutely nothing about him that should have scared her. And yet he did. A chill went down Ellie's spine. She found herself taking a step back as soon as he let go of her hand. Then, again without meaning to, she edged toward Hal, instinctively seeking his protection.

"Goddammit!" Hal's yell made her jump. He slammed his hands into the wall on either side of Shane. "What the hell is wrong with you?"

Shane didn't flinch or reply.

Confused, Ellie began, "He didn't do anything..."

"Yes, he did!" Hal growled. "Shane, you fucking apologize to my girl."

Her bewilderment was replaced with an irresistible wash of happiness. *My girl.* She'd already guessed it, with the whole "Meet the family" thing, but Hal had actually said it now. Impossible as it seemed, fast as it had happened, the bond between her and Hal was real. It wasn't just her who felt possessive of him, who wanted him to be hers and hers alone. He felt the same way about her.

There was a long pause while Hal and Shane had a stare-down contest.

"Put your hands down," Shane said at last. When Hal dropped his hands and stepped aside, Shane turned to Ellie. "I apologize."

"For what? You didn't do anything. I just..." She didn't want to admit that she'd gotten scared by absolutely nothing. It made her feel like a crazy person.

Then the penny dropped. Obviously, Shane had been hazing her, just like Nick and Rafa had. Only instead of verbally or physically challenging her, he'd deliberately frightened by her by sheer... power of will, or something. Her confusion was replaced by anger, then curiosity.

"How do you do that?" Ellie asked.

"Natural talent," Shane replied.

The team was all smiling at her or shooting irritated looks at Shane. It seemed like she'd passed their tests, even if Shane *had* managed to scare her. Maybe it was a "best falls out of three" thing.

As if Shane had read her mind, he said, "You passed my test too. Most people would have run."

Ellie turned back to the last three animal photos. She knew she didn't need to prove anything any more, but she wanted a more decisive win than "backed away instead of outright fleeing in terror." And also, she wanted to know if she was right.

"Nick's the wolf. He fights for dominance, but he respects a show of courage. Shane's the panther, lying in wait." Ellie felt her face crack into a smile as she concluded, "Hal's the grizzly bear. Strong. Protective. And really fucking big."

Shane nodded. "You got it."

Nick, Fiona, and Lucas applauded.

Destiny burst out laughing. "Big in more ways than one, right?"

"Look at him blush!" Rafa said. "Like a sweet, virginal maiden."

"You're all fired," said Hal, who was indeed blushing. But he was laughing too. He put his arm around her. "Sorry about this crazy crew of mine. If your brother decides to have his entire platoon of Marines run *me* through a gauntlet, I'll deserve it."

Ellie looked out at them. Not one of them seemed surprised that Hal was embracing his client. He'd obviously told them all in advance—hence the welcoming committee.

Just like me calling Catalina, she thought. *He was so happy, he'd just had to share the news.*

The ice broken, the team came up to casually chat with Ellie and Hal. Soon she was laughing and talking with them, completely at ease. It was like hanging out with a bunch of paramedics, or with Ethan's Marine buddies. They all had the camaraderie that comes of working closely together in a dangerous, exciting job, when you have to depend on your teammates to help you save a life… or to save yours.

They ordered in a lavish lunch, and ate it in a big conference room with picture windows overlooking the city. Huge storm clouds hung overhead, black and ominous, but no rain fell. Ellie was glad to be indoors, with Hal and his team, rather than at work.

After lunch, she stepped aside, took out her new disposable phone, and texted Catalina, *Hal took me to meet his family! (His team, actually. But same deal.)*

Catalina texted back, **No way! This soon?**

Ellie wrote, *Sometimes you just know.*

Any of them hot and single?

Hot: YES. Single: Don't know but there's 4 guys, no wedding rings. So probably at least one.

4!!!!!!!!!!!!!!!!!!!!!!! What are they like?

Ellie made sure no one was peeking over her shoulder as she wrote, **1 tatted bad boy (reminds me of Ethan.) 1 hot stud (and he knows it.) 1 foreign royalty (yes, seriously.) 1 quiet and scary (but in a hot way.)**

Instantly, Catalina replied, **Can I meet them? All of them.**

I'll ask.

Pls ask TACTFULLY. Don't make me sound desperate!!!!!!

Smiling, Ellie wrote, *Will do. Talk to you later.*

When she returned to the table, the team said their good-byes and took off, leaving Hal and Ellie alone.

"I like your family," she said.

Hal gave her a wry smile. "I'm not sure they all deserve it, but I'm glad. I'm sorry about the hazing. I had no idea they were going to do that."

"I think being over-protective comes with the job."

"I protect them," Hal said, frowning. "They don't need to protect me."

"Well, they obviously care a lot about you."

Hal, apparently uncomfortable with the entire subject, said, "Let's go back to my place. If you make a list of whatever else you want to get from your apartment, I can have my team collect it and bring it over, and then we can set it up. I don't want you to feel like you're living in a hotel."

"Sounds good."

They left Protection, Inc., and got into Hal's car. He took a completely different route back to his apartment than he'd taken to get there, frequently checking in his rear view mirror.

"Anybody following us?" Ellie asked, anxiety tingling up her nerves.

"No. I'll let you know if anyone does." He patted her hand. "Just so you know, this is an armored car, like the vans banks use to transport money. The windows are bullet-proof glass. And no one but my team knows where I live."

"Oh. Good." She relaxed. Hal would protect her. She was probably safer now, in his capable hands, than she'd been without a hit on her, just living a normal life alone in the city.

They arrived at his parking garage, and he pulled in. Hal scanned the garage before he got out of the car.

The elevator door slid open, revealing three men holding guns.

"Get down!" Hal shouted.

He threw himself in front of Ellie.

BANG!

53

CHAPTER FIVE
Hal

The impact took Hal full in the chest, knocking him backward. He yanked his gun from its holster and fired, even as a second bullet whistled past his ear. One of the hit men dropped where he stood.

Even with his armor, the impact hurt like hell. But Hal barely noticed through the red haze of adrenaline and rage.

Protect your mate! Hal's bear roared.

Keeping his body between Ellie and the hit men, Hal fired rapidly. The second hit man's shot went wild as he fell; Hal heard it strike concrete. An instant later, a searing pain tore through Hal's side.

Ricochet, Hal thought. The bullet must have bounced up and gone under his vest.

But he had no time to worry about himself. So long as he protected his mate, nothing else mattered.

Hal and the last hit man fired simultaneously. Another brutal impact slammed into Hal's chest. And the last hit man dropped, his gun falling from his hand.

Hal didn't need to check to make sure the enemies were dead; while they'd taken the easier center-of-mass shots, he'd aimed at their unprotected heads.

In the blink of an eye it took him to spin around and look for Ellie, Hal died a thousand deaths. If he'd been too slow— If he'd failed— if his mate was dead—

Ellie was alive and breathing, frightened but unhurt.

"Hal!" Ellie gasped. "Were you hit?"

He didn't have time for that. "Hold on."

Hal scanned the parking lot again. Nothing. It was clear.

"Get back in the car!" Hal grabbed her arm and ran with her, keeping his body between her and the gate.

He pushed her into the passenger seat, slammed the door, and dove into the driver's seat. Then he hit the code to open the gate, and floored it out of there.

Hal gritted his teeth, one hand clenched tight on the steering wheel and one pressed to his side. The gunshot wound burned like he'd been stabbed with a red-hot poker. Hot blood was soaking through his shirt and pants and even his heavy overcoat. Luckily the wound was in his left side. From the passenger seat, Ellie might notice that he was holding his hand to his side, but she wouldn't be able to see the wet spot.

"Are you hurt?" Ellie demanded. "Hal, answer me!"

"No." He couldn't have her fussing over him while he was trying to make sure they weren't being followed.

Fear and frustration sharpened her voice as she said, "Then why are you clutching at your side? Hal, I know you took a hit!"

"It hit my vest. I think the impact cracked a few ribs." Hal spoke on auto-pilot. He'd say anything to give himself space to protect her, and deal with the consequences later.

"Oh." Ellie sounded relieved. "Yeah, that hurts a lot. I could tape them for you later."

"Sure. Thanks." He checked the rear view mirrors again. "No one's following us."

Ellie put her hand on his shoulder. "Hal, you saved my life. I know thank you doesn't even begin to cover it, but… Thank you."

It made him feel a little better. No matter what else he lost, he hadn't lost his mate.

The sky was iron gray, the storm clouds massed and ominous. He got on the freeway, heading out of the city.

"Aren't you going to Protection, Inc.?" Ellie asked.

"No," Hal said. He knew he had to explain, but his jaw felt stuck.

The pain in his heart far outweighed the pain in his side. He'd known what had to have happened the instant he'd seen the hit men in the elevator. But saying it aloud made it feel more real.

"Hal, what's wrong?" Ellie seemed to hear what she'd just said, and added, "I mean, apart from us both getting shot at."

"I know what you mean." He unlocked his jaw. He had to tell her. "Someone told those hit men where I live. The only people who know where I live are you and my team."

Ellie stared at him. "You think someone on your team sold you out?"

"I don't want to believe that. But I have to consider the possibility."

"Which one could it be?"

Hal winced. There was something else he didn't want to think of. Even considering them as traitors made him feel like a traitor to *them*. "Well... Lucas is new. I don't know him as well as the others. Nick has a shady background. Fiona has a different sort of shady background. And Shane's isn't even shady. It's more like pitch black."

"What about Rafa?" Ellie asked. "There's no way he'd betray you, right? You said he was your best friend!"

"No, Rafa would never—" Hal began, then stopped. "Well... I hate to say this, but I can think of one reason he might. And the same goes for Destiny. They both have family they're really close to. Including little kids. If Nagle threatened Destiny's baby brother or Rafa's nieces..."

Ellie looked as dismayed as Hal felt. "Isn't there any other way someone could have found out?"

"Oh, sure." As Hal listed off the possibilities, he prayed that one of them was true. "I missed someone following me there. Or one of my team missed someone. They're all very competent, but anyone can screw up once. And once Nagle knew where to find me, he could hire a hacker to get his men inside. But... I can't risk contacting my team yet. Not till I know more. Ellie, I can't risk you."

She leaned over and kissed his cheek. The butterfly brush of her lips brought him some comfort.

More than anything else, he wanted to tell her he was hit, and let her tend his wounds and hold him in her arms. He wanted it so badly, it made his heart hurt that he couldn't have it.

But she was a paramedic. And while he wasn't sure how badly he was injured, he could feel that he was bleeding a lot. She'd take one look at all that blood, and demand that he go to a hospital. And if he was in a hospital, he couldn't protect her.

Shifters healed faster and better than humans. Hal was reasonably certain that he didn't need a hospital. But he couldn't explain that to Ellie without explaining that he was a shifter.

He bit his lip, wishing he'd already told her. She practically already knew— maybe not literally, but she'd correctly guessed everyone's shift forms from the photos at Protection, Inc. If he could sit her down in a calm atmosphere and gently explain it, he was pretty sure she'd be surprised but not frightened or horrified.

Evading hit men in a speeding car, while they were both already shaken up and coming off a murder attempt, while he was wounded and bleeding and barely able to get his thoughts together, was the opposite of a calm atmosphere. God knew how she'd take it. She'd probably think he was delirious. And he had to get as far from town as fast as possible. He couldn't afford to lose time by pulling over and hiking into the forest to demonstrate.

"Where are we going?" Ellie asked.

"A cabin in the woods," Hal replied, relieved at the easy question. "My family owns it, but no one's there now. And only my family knows about it, so it's safe."

"Oh. Okay." She peered into his face, looking worried. "Do you want to stop now, and have me tape up your ribs? You look like you're in a lot of pain. And I'd like to examine you. A blow hard enough to crack ribs could have caused internal injuries."

Hal was touched at her concern. "You can check me once we get there. I want to get out of here as fast as I can."

"Let me know if you start feeling dizzy or sick or short of breath, or if the pain gets worse."

"Okay."

Hal did feel dizzy and sick and short of breath, and the pain *was* getting worse. But he could take it. He was strong and tough. He was a shifter. And he'd do anything to protect his mate.

Hold on, his bear rumbled. *Keep your mate safe.*

Hal pressed his hand tighter against his side, and drove on.

CHAPTER SIX
Ellie

Hal was silent as he sped along the freeway, his body tense and his rugged features taut with pain. As they passed the city limits, a hard rain began to fall. Ellie huddled in her seat, cold despite the hot air coming through the heating system. Now that the initial shock had worn off, the reality of what had happened was sinking in.

Nagle had tried to kill her, and had nearly succeeded.

If Hal was right, he'd been betrayed by one of his own team members. No wonder he was so quiet and grim. The thought of it saddened her, and she'd only just met them. It had to be ten times more of a blow to Hal, who thought of them like his family.

If Nagle could get to Hal's own team, Ellie really wasn't safe in Santa Martina. She might not be safe anywhere.

Ellie stared blankly out the window, lost in depressing thoughts. She barely noticed as the city streets gave way to broad highways cutting through fields, then narrow highways cutting through a forest. The rain turned to hail, clattering off the roof and windshield like thrown pebbles. Finally snow began to fall. The white flakes fell lightly at first, then more heavily. The black strip of highway became salt-and-pepper, and then pure white.

Ellie turned to Hal to ask him if he had snow chains for the tires. The road must be getting slick and treacherous with ice and snow.

"Do you—" She broke off, staring at him.

Hal's tanned face had gone pale. Though the car was merely warm, he was sweating heavily. He stared straight ahead, eyes glassy and jaw clenched. His entire body was stiff with pain, his right hand locked around the steering wheel in a death grip and his left still pressed to his side. Now that the loud clatter of hail had turned to the silent fall of snow, she could hear him breathing, shallow and fast.

Ellie's heart stuttered with fear. Hal's injuries had to be more serious than he'd realized.

"You *are* hurt."

"Just the cracked ribs." His voice was strained.

"Do they normally make you sweat like that?" Ellie touched his cheek. His skin was cold, a sign of shock. She put a finger beneath his jaw, feeling for his pulse.

He tried to pull his head aside. "Stop it. I'm fine."

She kept her fingers where they were, though they slid against the cold sweat that drenched his skin. His pulse was weak; she had to press hard to feel it all. When she did locate it, she didn't need to check her watch to know that it was too fast.

"Pull over," Ellie said. "I need to examine you. I think you have internal injuries."

"Can't. Have to keep going."

Anger surged through her. Hal must have known for some time that the bullet had done more damage than cracked ribs, but he'd said nothing while she'd uselessly sat and stared out the window, refusing to let her help him even though she was completely qualified to do so. Didn't he trust her at all?

"Goddammit, Hal, pull over," Ellie demanded. "I'm a paramedic. I know what I'm doing."

"I know," Hal replied. She could hear now how hard it was for him to talk. "But I need to get you to safety. We're almost there. You can check me when we arrive."

"We've already wasted too much time," Ellie retorted, frustrated and worried. "Hal, what part of 'internal bleeding' did you not understand? You need to go to a hospital. Immediately."

He shook his head, wincing. "I can't. Nagle's men might be there. It wouldn't be safe for you."

Ellie couldn't believe her ears. "For me? Safe for *me?* Forget me! You could *die!*"

Hal pried one hand off the steering wheel to touch her shoulder. He probably meant it to be a reassuring pat, but his hand was clumsy and graceless. It smacked into her shoulder, then slid down and hung limp at his side. He leaned forward, blinking and frowning at the road ahead.

"It's so dark," he muttered.

The snow was falling hard, making it hard to see much beyond whirling white, but the light was no dimmer than it had been a minute ago.

Darkening vision. Loss of coordination. Probable internal injuries.

"Hal, pull over right now!" Ellie's voice rose in a shout. "You're passing out!"

Hal's gaze snapped into focus. "Oh, shit."

He turned the wheel to steer for the side of the road, and she saw his foot start to move from the gas pedal to the brake. Then his foot dropped, his hand fell to his side, and his eyes closed. Before she could catch him, he pitched forward over the steering wheel.

The horn blasted and kept on blaring. Ellie tried to push Hal back, then aside, but he was much too heavy for her to move. Her heart pounding, she caught the edge of the wheel and steadied it, steering the car along the deserted highway.

Much as she desperately wanted to check Hal's breathing and pulse, she had to get the car stopped first. She couldn't help him if they were both killed in a crash. Keeping a firm grip on the wheel, she managed to work her left leg up and over until she could kick his foot off the gas. Then she slowly braked as she steered the car toward the side of the road.

The car slowed, hit a bump that made her heart lurch, then came to a stop off road. She put it in park and turned off the engine. The silence was so complete that Ellie felt like she'd gone deaf. She fumbled for Hal's pulse and was tremendously relieved when she felt it, beating faint but steadily beneath her fingers.

Ellie hit the button to tilt Hal's seat back. She supported his head and eased him down with the seat, until he was lying almost flat. Then she tipped back her own seat, so both seats were like side-by-side benches.

"Thank God for luxury cars," Ellie muttered. Her own cheap-mobile had seats that tilted about six inches either way.

Hal didn't stir, but lay still with his eyes closed and his strong hands slack. It was scary to see him so vulnerable, when he'd always been so strong and protective.

She unbuttoned his black overcoat, then pulled it open. The shirt beneath his coat was soaked in blood.

"Son of a bitch!" Ellie yelled.

Hal's eyelashes fluttered, and his hazel eyes slowly opened. He looked confused for a moment, and then she saw memory return.

"Sorry." His voice was a low rumble, barely audible.

She unbuttoned his shirt, then unstrapped the heavy vest. "Some bulletproof vest! You ought to sue."

Hal tried to smile, despite his pain. "The vest worked fine. A ricochet went under it."

Ellie eased the vest off, then took a pair of scissors from her purse and sheared off his undershirt. There were two huge black bruises on his chest where bullets had struck the armor plates. But she was more concerned about the wounds in his side, just above his hip. The bullet had gone through and through, leaving a small entrance wound and a larger exit wound. Both were still bleeding, though slowly.

"Is there a first aid kit in the car?" Ellie asked.

"In the trunk."

She lifted his hand and held it to the wounds. "Keep pressure on them."

He pressed his hand against his side, wincing. Ellie remembered how he'd steered with one hand for the entire trip, keeping his other hand tight against his side. And how he'd claimed that it was because he had cracked ribs.

She bit her lip against yelling at him, much as she was tempted to. He didn't need her scolding him right now. "I'll get the kit."

She turned on the ignition and cranked the heat to maximum. Hal needed to stay as warm as possible. Then she hit the button to release the trunk and opened the car door. The blast of frigid air made her shiver even before she got out.

Her feet sank into snow, nearly up to her ankles. Alarmed, Ellie took a look at the car. Not only was snow piling up around the car, but the rear tires had sunk deep into either a pothole or a mud-hole.

Shit.

She needed to treat Hal as quickly as possible, then drive him to the nearest hospital before they got trapped by the falling snow. Ellie could only pray that they weren't trapped already.

She hurried to the back of the car. The trunk was thoroughly stocked, as if Hal had been preparing for a zombie apocalypse, crammed full of easy-carry trunks with labels like FIRST AID, GENERAL SUPPLIES, and FOOD AND WATER. She grabbed a FIRST AID trunk and two folded blankets, then scrambled back into the car.

She was relieved to find that Hal was still conscious. Ellie checked him again, surprised but pleased to find that his skin was warmer, his breathing easier, and his pulse slower. It was amazing how sometimes something as simple as turning up the heat could help so much. It undoubtedly also helped that Hal was strong and fit.

"You're tough," she said.

He tried to smile. "Sorry I scared you. I'll be fine. I promise."

"You better be, you macho idiot," she retorted as she opened the first aid kit. "Would it have killed you to tell me you got *shot*?"

"You would've tried to drag me to a hospital. Nagle's men would have tracked us there, and I wouldn't have been able to protect—"

Ellie swabbed antiseptic over Hal's wounds. He broke off, gritting his teeth against the pain. "What about a private hospital? They're much more discreet."

"I don't need any hospital."

"Yes, you do," Ellie repeated, with emphasis. She applied pressure bandages to the wounds, stopping the bleeding. "Unless you've got IV fluids and oxygen and an X-Ray machine and maybe an anesthesiologist and a surgeon stashed in the trunk?"

Hal gave her a frustrated glance. "I told you, I'll be fine. I just need a little rest. But we need to get out of here—" As she opened her mouth, he quickly said, "Not to a hospital! To my cabin. You drive. I'll direct you."

Ellie closed her mouth. This argument could obviously go on forever, and there was no time to waste. Once she was in the driver's seat, she could take him wherever she liked. "Fine."

"Let's switch seats."

That was easier said than done. Though Hal's car was big and roomy, he was a huge guy and too badly hurt to move easily. Ellie worried that he wouldn't be able to sit up at all, but once she got her arms under his shoulders, she was able to help him up. Once he was sitting up, he leaned against her, breathing hard.

"Sorry," he said. "Just give me a second."

"Take as much time as you need," Ellie replied, squeezing his broad shoulders. "You've been *shot*. Give yourself a break."

He didn't reply. His silky hair mingled with hers, their heads pressed together. She could feel his chest rise and fall as he breathed. His muscles were hard as steel, tensed with pain.

Ellie rubbed his back in slow circles, hoping that would ease his pain. Since she intended to deliver him to a hospital, like it or not, she didn't want to offer him any painkillers. They'd assess him again there, and a doctor could decide what sort of medication he needed. Besides, he'd undoubtedly refuse any drug that might knock him out.

Hal's deep voice rumbled in her ear. "Okay. Let's switch."

She supported him as he moved from the driver's seat to the passenger seat, then helped him lie back down in it. Then she took off his shoes, to make him more comfortable.

But when she reached to unbuckle his belt, he raised a hand to stop her. "My gun."

The holster was attached to his belt.

"Okay. I'll leave it." She covered him with the blankets she'd gotten from the trunk, thinking that he wouldn't even be able to draw his gun, let alone fire it. But if it made him feel better to keep wearing it, he could wear it.

Hal reached up with one big hand and cupped her cheek. As always, it was startling how gentle his touch could be. She started to lean into his warm caress, but he lowered his arm to his side as if it was too heavy to hold up for so long.

"I should've…" he mumbled. His voice trailed off.

She caught his hand between hers. "Rest, Hal."

"Ellie… I should've…" His lips parted as if he meant to say more. Then he closed his eyes.

Uncertain whether he'd passed out or was simply resting, she pressed a kiss onto his forehead. He didn't so much as smile. Passed out, for sure.

She slid into the driver's seat, hit the button to raise the back, and turned the key in the ignition. The engine raced as she pressed down on the gas, but the car didn't move. The wheels were stuck fast in the mud.

"Goddammit!" Ellie exclaimed.

She stepped on the gas again, but though she could feel the wheels spinning and see mud and snow flying, the car didn't budge.

She checked her cell phone, then Hal's. No service. They were too far out in the country. And they were stuck there unless she could flag down someone to call them a tow truck.

Ellie could barely see the country road through the snow, and she doubted any passing car would even see their car, let alone realize that they were stuck rather than simply parked. If she wanted to get help, she'd have to leave the car, stand by the side of the road, and cross her fingers that a car came by before she succumbed to hypothermia.

And also, that the car contained innocent passers-by rather than a bunch of Nagle's hit men.

She frowned down at Hal, wondering which he would advise. He was the security expert, after all. And while he'd obviously recommend whatever he thought was safest for her, not what was best for himself, there were dangers for her either way. Once the gas ran out, the car would get very cold, very quickly. She'd seen enough hypothermia victims to know that.

"Hal. Wake up, Hal." She squeezed his hand, harder and harder until he drew in a deep breath and opened his eyes. "I need to ask you something."

He looked exhausted, but his eyes were more focused than they'd been a minute ago. "Okay."

She briefly outlined the problem.

"Out of the frying pan, into the fire, huh?" Hal said. But to her relief, he didn't seem too worried. "Don't try to flag down a car. We've got plenty of gas. If we turn on the engine for fifteen minutes every hour, the car will stay warm enough. I can push it out of the mud once I feel better."

"Hal," Ellie said gently. "It'll be a couple weeks before you're up to *pushing a car*."

"No. It'll be tomorrow. Listen, Ellie." He caught her hand. His fingers were warm and dry, and some strength had returned to his grip. "You were right. I should've told you I was hit. And there's something else I should've told you. I was afraid to, I guess. But I'm going to trust that no matter how shocked you are, you won't run away without giving me a chance to explain."

That sounded ominous. Trying not to sound alarmed, Ellie said, "Why don't you tell me now? I'm not the running away type. I guess unless you're a serial killer."

"I'm not a serial killer," Hal said, and she heard a touch of amusement in his voice. Then he visibly geared up for what he had to say next. Finally, he said, "But I am a bear shifter."

Ellie wasn't sure she'd heard him right. "A what? What is that?"

"A bear shifter," he repeated. "Uh… I turn into a bear. You know, like a werewolf? But a bear. A werebear."

"A werebear," Ellie repeated.

She wished she could believe he was joking, but he seemed completely serious. He'd said "I'm a bear shifter" like a teenager might say, "I'm gay," or a woman might say, "I'm pregnant."

It was much too early for infection to have set into his wounds and given him a fever, but it was possible to become delirious from shock and blood loss alone. It was a bad sign.

She stroked his hair, trying not to let the fear she felt for him show in her voice. "Okay. It's fine, Hal. Don't worry about it."

"I'm not delirious." Hal caught her hand and pulled it down to his lips. He kissed it, then said, "Just remember, I would never hurt you."

What he did next took her completely by surprise. He flung the car door open and half stepped, half fell outside.

"Hal!" Ellie shouted.

He held out a hand. "Stay there!"

Then something impossible happened.

Hal's body swelled enormously. His pants and the bandages around his chest ripped off. Shaggy brown fur sprang up. Before Ellie could so much as gasp, Hal was gone and a huge grizzly bear stood in his place.

The bear stuck his head into the car and nuzzled Ellie's hand. Dazed, she automatically petted it. His fur was thick and soft.

The grizzly raised his head, looking at Ellie with hazel eyes. Brown as earth, green as leaves. The bear had Hal's eyes.

"Hal?" Ellie's voice came out in a whisper.

The bear nodded his giant head. Then he shrank. Fur receded, replaced by tanned skin. In the blink of an eye, the grizzly was gone.

Hal knelt naked in the snow, blood trickling down his side.

Ellie leaped to help him back into the car. He was shivering, his bare skin chilled. She'd never have been able to lift him by herself, but he managed to stagger back into the car and collapse into the passenger seat.

She slammed the door, but the damage had been done. The car was freezing inside. She turned on the engine. Hot air began to blow, warming the interior.

"Macho. Idiot!" Ellie glared down at Hal. "You're bleeding again."

"Didn't... Didn't think about that." His teeth were chattering; he could hardly get the words out.

She snatched up the first aid kit, quickly cleaned the wounds again, and re-bandaged them. But it was too familiar a task to fully occupy her mind.

Bear shifter.

Werebear.

"Shane's the panther, lying in wait. Hal's the grizzly bear."

As she wrapped blankets around him, she asked, "Is Lucas really a dragon... A dragon shifter... a weredragon?"

Hal nodded. To her relief, his shivering had subsided.

"And Nick's a werewolf."

"Yeah." Hal gazed at her with his gorgeous hazel eyes. His bear's eyes. "I didn't know how to tell you. I wanted to wait for the perfect moment."

"That sure as hell wasn't it!"

"No," Hal admitted. "But it's why I didn't want to go to the hospital. I really don't need to. Shifters heal fast. I'm not in any danger, Ellie. In a day or so, I'll have completely recovered."

"Oh." It took a moment to sink in. Hal wasn't going to bleed to death or die of shock. She wasn't going to lose him. He wouldn't die.

To her surprise, a sob tore up from deep in her chest. Then another. Burning tears ran down her face. She couldn't control them, or the ugly sounds she heard herself making. She tried to turn away, to hide herself, even though she knew it was too late. But a hand caught her wrist.

"Hey." Hal's deep voice tugged at her attention with more strength than his grip on her arm. "I wore myself out with that stunt. I can't sit up and hold you. Come lie down next to me."

The car was built on a larger-than-life scale, or she never could have managed it. Even with both of them lying on their sides, it was a tight fit. But she lay down next to Hal, pulled the blankets over them, and cried on his shoulder. He held her tight, his body heat and presence soothing her.

"It's all right," he murmured. "It's all right."

At first she was embarrassed, and then she stopped caring. Hal was alive. He'd saved her, but he hadn't traded his life for hers, as she'd feared.

"I thought you'd die," she whispered. "In the parking lot, when you threw yourself in front of me. In the car, when I saw that you were hit. When I realized the car was trapped. People *die* of cold and shock and blood loss. Especially all three together!"

Hal pulled her in even closer, wiping her tears away. "I'm sorry, Ellie. I was so wrapped up in protecting you, I didn't stop to think what it was like *for* you."

"I was going to drive you to the emergency room, like it or not," she admitted.

The rumble of his chuckle vibrated through her body. "I figured. That's why I had to let you know. And my bear can't fit in the car."

"Your bear," she repeated, marveling. "Did a werebear bite you? Or were you born that way?"

"I was born a bear shifter. When I said my family was back to nature… Well, they're *really* back to nature. I come from a clan of grizzly bears that don't like the city or cars or television. It was a big deal when they bought a refrigerator. I was the black sheep."

Ellie's face cracked in a fragile smile. "Black bear."

"We've got some of those in the clan, too."

She wiped her eyes on her hands. "What about Protection, Inc.? Are they all black sheep, too?"

"One way or another." His muscles tensed against hers. "Damn, nearly forgot. My gun's outside. Can you get it?"

Ellie reluctantly extracted herself, went outside, and retrieved the gun and holster. Hal snatched them up and set them on the floor, within hand's reach. He was still thinking of protecting her, though she couldn't imagine that even Nagle's hit men would venture out in this storm.

"I know how to shoot," she said. "I mean, not like you. But Ethan taught me. You don't have to stay up and guard me. Let me take a turn guarding you."

Hal's expression was priceless. Then he gave a rueful shrug. "All right. I trust you. And I'll heal faster if I rest. But wake me up the second you think anything might be wrong, okay?"

"I will." Ellie bent down and kissed him. "Sleep like a… bear. Do werebears hibernate?"

"My grandpa might. Hard to tell." He drifted off before she could ask him if he was joking.

She sat and watched over him, sometimes stroking his soft hair. The moon shone through the clouds and snow, casting a pale light.

Ellie had so much to think about, it was easy to stay awake. Were-wolves and other were-creatures were real. *Dragons* were real. Hal could turn into a bear. It was all impossible and amazing, miracles come to shaggy-furred life.

But none of it was more marvelous than the rise and fall of Hal's chest beneath her hand. He was alive, and he loved her. And she loved him. Nothing could be more of a miracle than that.

CHAPTER SEVEN
Hal

Ellie spoke in an urgent whisper. "Hal!"

Hal woke in a flash, instantly aware of where he was and what had happened. He prevented himself from jumping up by sheer force of will; the last thing Ellie needed was for him to pass out again. But he did snatch his gun out of the holster. "What's happening?"

"I'm not sure." But her voice was low; something had alarmed her. "I heard a car coming, from the direction of Santa Martina. It pulled off the road and parked somewhere pretty far behind us. I'd only just started to hear it when I heard it stop."

Hal was calculating the odds of staying in the car, which was armored and bulletproof, versus leaving it, when Ellie went on, "But it's probably not Nagle's guys. I've heard other cars pass. If anyone saw us, they probably would have pulled over to see if we need help. I don't think we're visible from the road."

At her words, Hal suddenly understood exactly what was going on. He knew who was in the car, how he and Ellie had been tracked, and how the hit men had learned where he'd lived. And he knew, too, why they'd waited till the middle of the night to go after him and Ellie.

"Open the driver's door, just as far as you need to so you can get out," Hal whispered urgently. "Leave your purse. Crawl out, then crawl on your belly toward the woods, as fast as you can. I'll be right behind you. Go!"

To his relief, she didn't hesitate. She was out the door in a flash, wriggling through the snow like a boot camp recruit in an obstacle course. Hal got a good grip on his gun, then followed her.

The snow was painful against the half-healed wounds in his side, the air in his lungs shockingly cold. The moon had set, and even his sharper-than-human vision could barely make out a thing. He caught up with Ellie and tugged her along, dragging her through the snow faster than she could go by herself. His heart pounded. He had no idea if they'd been seen leaving the car, or how long they had to get away if they hadn't.

The forest rose up before them like a black wall. Hal hauled Ellie into its shelter, then stopped and turned back. The car they'd left was visible as a black silhouette in a field of white.

BOOM!

The explosion shattered the still of the night. A blast of hot air buffeted him as the car blew up in a fireball. Ellie gasped, but there was no way anyone farther than him could hear anything over the roar of flames.

He reached out until he found her lips, and put his finger across them, feeling its softness and her nod; she understood. Then, to his immense relief, he heard the sound of an engine turning over, and a car speeding away. No figures attempted to creep across the field of snow.

"They're gone," Hal said. His voice sounded shockingly loud in his own ears. "They think we're dead."

"What *was* that?" Ellie gasped.

"An RPG— a rocket-propelled grenade."

"Did you know that would happen?"

"Sort of," he replied. "I figured out a lot of things in a flash, when you told me about the car. They waited till the middle of the night and parked way back because they were going to do something really spectacular— something they could only get away with if no one was around. If we can't be seen from the road, then they had to have tracked us here. When you were at the police station, did they take anything that belonged to you and then give it back?"

"My purse." Ellie stared at him. "Was it bugged? Are the cops in on it?"

"Maybe just one cop. Do you remember who took it?"

"Detective Kramer. Now that I think about it, he said a lot of stuff that was probably meant to scare me off testifying. He tried to keep me from talking to the watch commander, too, but I insisted."

"Good thing you did," Hal said. "The watch commander was the one who called me. And yeah, I think Kramer stuck a tracker in your purse. Now I feel like an asshole, suspecting my own team."

"I'm glad it's not them."

Heartfelt, Hal said, "Me too. I owe them."

"I owe *you*," Ellie said. "You saved my life. Again."

"Don't forget that you kept watch and noticed when something suspicious happened. You saved my life, too. But don't make a habit of it. That's supposed to be my job. I'm too young to retire."

As he'd hoped, his joking eased the strain of yet another near-death experience. She laughed, a little giddily.

As the adrenaline rush faded, he became very conscious of how cold he was, stark naked in the snow and icy air. He shivered.

Ellie must have felt it, because she said, "We've got to find shelter. You'll freeze."

"Grizzlies like this sort of weather. *You're* the one I'm worried about." His lips were starting to get numb. He spoke hastily, while he still could. "I'll shift and lead you to the cabin. It's not that far."

"Okay." She sounded calm again.

His heart swelled with love of his brave, steady, caring girl. How had he ever imagined that his mate would tie him down? She didn't burden him or hinder him, she lifted him and carried him farther than he could go alone. Being mated wasn't being trapped, it was being set free.

"I love you," Hal said.

She fumbled for his face, then caught it in both hands and kissed him. "I love you too. You always take me on such exciting dates."

He chuckled, then handed her the gun. "Carry this for me."

Hal focused on being a bear. A bear's simple thoughts and compelling instincts and sharp senses...

He transformed. The world jumped into clearer view. Scents rose up strong and vivid, of damp earth, moss, and dead leaves. Ellie's tempting natural scent was stronger, too. He could see the tall trees and thick snow, and Ellie, huddled and shivering beside him. The air was still frigid, but he was warm beneath his thick fur. He wished he could loan it to her.

He nudged her with his head and set off for his cabin. She walked beside him, her hands buried in his fur.

At first she talked to him, but soon her teeth chattered too much for that, and she fell silent. She was dressed for a cool day, not for a long trek in freezing weather, trudging along in ankle-deep snow. If she was out too long, she'd get hypothermic, exactly as she'd worried he would.

Hal walked faster, trying to hurry her up, but soon had to abandon the attempt. She couldn't see as well as he could, and had to walk slowly, feeling her way with her feet, or she'd trip. The last thing she needed was a broken ankle.

He tried to keep close to her, to share the warmth of his fur, but it was a losing battle against the freezing night. Ellie became slower and slower, frequently stumbling. Her feet must be numb with cold, her face aching with it, but she didn't complain. Her shivering slowed, then stopped.

Fear chilled Hal's heart. He wasn't a paramedic, but Navy SEALs were taught how to survive in extreme conditions… and how to know if the environment was about to kill you. She hadn't stopped shivering because she was getting warmer, she'd stopped because her body had given up on trying to warm her and was trying to conserve energy instead.

She stumbled again, then collapsed in the snow.

Hal became a man and knelt beside her. "Ellie!"

She didn't stir. He laid his hand on her chest, and felt it rise with her breathing. She was alive, but hypothermic. He had to get her to the cabin, where he could warm her up.

As a bear, he couldn't carry her. As a man, he was naked and barefoot and in danger of freezing himself, not to mention that he could barely see. But he had no choice. Hal hoisted her over his shoulder, and set off through the woods.

A minute later, he realized that he'd left without his gun, but he didn't dare waste time going back to search for it. His bare feet burned with cold, then went numb, followed by the rest of his body. Tree branches he didn't see smacked him across the face, and though he was too numb to feel pain, he did feel the blood run down hot, then freeze. But he could feel his mate breathing, and that was all he needed to keep him going.

The light slowly brightened as he set a quick pace through the forest, going from black to gray to pearly white. When he finally emerged from the woods, the sun was rising. He could see his cabin, nestled into a hillside.

Hal set out at a run. He located the key, hidden within a hollow tree, and fumbled to open the door. His hands were clumsy, and he dropped the key twice. But he finally got the door open.

He kicked it shut behind him and jammed in the deadbolt, then laid Ellie down on the sofa and went to light the fire and the wood-burning stove that heated the little cabin.

When he returned to her, she was stirring. "Where are we?"

"The cabin."

She tried to sit up, but he picked her up instead. "I'll get you warmed up."

He carried her to the shower, thankful that his family believed in hot water, even if they didn't believe in central heating. Hal stripped off her clothes. They were wet and stiff, frozen near-solid in some places.

Then he stepped into the shower, still holding her in his arms, and let the warm water wash over them both. Under the cascading warmth, Ellie's skin went from pale to pink, and she stretched happily in his arms.

"Oh, this feels good," she murmured.

Hal gritted his teeth, not enjoying it nearly as much. The water burned and stung as his skin prickled back to life. He'd been numb from cold before, but now everything hurt: the cuts on his face, the deep bruises on his chest, the wounds in his side, and the soles of his feet. Especially his feet. They hurt so much, he could hardly stand up.

They could sit down under the water, but he was afraid that once he took the weight off his feet, he wouldn't be able to get up again. So he held his mate in his arms, feeling like he was balancing on razor blades, until he was sure that she was as warm as the water could get her.

She blinked up at him, looking more awake. "You're bleeding."

"I couldn't see very well. A bunch of branches hit me in the face."

"Put me down. I'll patch you up." She squirmed to get down, but Hal tightened his grip.

"It's nothing. You need to get under some warm blankets, and drink some hot tea."

"So do you," Ellie retorted. "You carried me here, didn't you? Naked through the snow."

Hal shrugged. "Well, yeah, but—"

"Is there a first aid kit here?"

"Yeah."

"Then bring it to the bed. With hot tea for both of us."

"You're bossy," he remarked.

"So are you."

They grinned at each other, amused rather than annoyed.

Hal turned off the shower and dried Ellie off first, then himself. Then he carried her to the bed, piled blankets over her, and went to the kitchen to make tea. While it was brewing, he got one of the disposable phones he kept in the cabin and called Rafa.

"Hal!" Rafa's yell made Hal pull the phone a little away from his ear. "What the hell is going on? Three of Nagle's hit men are dead in your garage. Are you all right?"

"I'm fine. And Ellie's fine. But I could use some help. I think Detective Kramer's working for Nagle." Hal filled Rafa in on what had happened, including his suspicion that Kramer had hidden a tracker in Ellie's purse.

"Shall we set up a sting?" Rafa asked.

"My thought exactly," Hal replied. "Give Nagle a few days to think we're dead and relax. Then call Kramer and tell him I contacted you. Tell him Ellie and I are in a safe house, and give him an address. Bug the hell out of it, and take the team to stake it out. See who shows up to kill me, and record whatever they say. Hopefully we'll get enough evidence to implicate Kramer and get Nagle held without bail."

"Will do. I'll call the team now. We were all worried about you, Hal."

A day or so, Hal would have brushed that off, uncomfortable with the idea of his team feeling protective of him. Now, he said, "Thanks, Rafa. Tell everyone I'm fine, and I appreciate it. And that I know they'll do a great job."

He hung up the phone, poured out the tea, and stirred lots of honey into it. By the time he returned to the bedroom with the tea and the first aid kit, his feet hurt so much that he couldn't stop himself from limping. It was a tremendous relief to crawl into bed, press his body up against hers, and drink the hot tea.

Ellie's sharp gaze clearly didn't miss a thing, but she didn't comment until she'd finished her tea. Then she said, "I know we haven't really talked about the future. And I know it's ridiculously soon. But I feel like we do have one."

"We do. Shifters mate for life." They were both sitting up, leaning back against the headboard. Hal put his arm around her shoulders. "The moment I saw you, I knew you were my mate. You've got me for as long as you want me. I hope that's forever."

Ellie leaned her head against his. "I'll always want you, Hal. You walked naked and barefoot through the snow for me! And then you brought me tea in bed. Forever it is."

They kissed, and then she said, "So if we're going to be together for good, there's something you'd better get used to. If you get hurt and it's something I can handle, I patch you up. No suffering in silence because you're too tough and strong to need anyone!"

Hal thought about that. It had been so automatic, trying not to let her see him limping until he could finish taking care of her. But some types of protection ended up hurting in the long run. He'd never forget the shock, pain, and anger in Ellie's eyes as she'd realized that he'd been bleeding for hours without letting her know he was hurt.

Over-protective bodyguard bear shifter meets crazy-brave paramedic, Hal thought. *We really do need each other.*

"You're used to taking care of everyone else before yourself, aren't you?" Hal said at last. "I'm used to protecting everyone else before myself. But I do need people. I need my team, and I'm sorry as hell that I doubted them. And I need you. So I'll take your deal. I'll let you protect me and take care of me, if you let me do the same for you."

Ellie's eyes glistened with unshed tears. Her voice was husky as she said, "All right. It's a deal."

"And in token of my sincerity…" Hal handed her the first aid kit and moved to lay his feet in her lap. "My feet are killing me. Patch me up."

She smiled at him, then drew in her breath as she looked down at his feet. He couldn't see the full extent of the damage, but what he could see of his soles was a mass of bruises, deep gashes, and frostbite.

"Shifter healing," he reminded her.

"Thank goodness for that. Otherwise, I'd be afraid you'd have to have some toes amputated. They look like you climbed Mount Everest barefoot." She ruffled his hair. "Lie down. I hope you're tired enough to fall asleep. Otherwise, this is going to hurt like hell."

Hal lay back, letting his mate go to work. She knew what she was doing, and he trusted her. He closed his eyes, and let his mate take care of him while he drifted off to sleep.

CHAPTER EIGHT
Ellie

Ellie and Hal spent most of the next few days recovering in bed. They were both exhausted, and despite Hal's shifter healing, it was some time before he could walk without pain. They did a lot of kissing and cuddling, but neither of them had the energy for anything more. They spent most of the time dozing or talking.

She would have expected to find the time boring and frustrating, but instead she found it cozy and healing. Ellie and Hal told each other stories, revealing their pasts and detailing their hopes for their future. When she slept, she dreamed of him.

But gradually, their energy returned. They began spending less time in bed, and more in the living room watching the snow fall or cooking in the kitchen.

To Ellie's relief, there was a stash of clothing in the attic that fit her. It mostly consisted of dresses rather than her usual jeans and blouses, but she was so relieved to have something to wear other than the one outfit she'd ruined crawling around in the woods that she didn't mind.

"Shifters always have lots of extra clothing around," Hal explained with a laugh. "For obvious reasons. It's considered basic hospitality to keep clothes in sizes you don't wear, in case a friend or relative needs an emergency outfit."

Hal had a trunk full of his own emergency clothing as well. To Ellie's amusement, she spotted a box of condoms buried at the bottom.

"Oh, so you've brought girlfriends here before," she teased.

Hal shook his head. "I just lived in hope."

They were in the kitchen, with Ellie chopping potatoes and Hal peeling carrots for a stew, when Hal's phone rang.

He put down the peeler and picked it up. "Hello?"

She watched as his face shifted from interest to excitement to exultation. "Thanks. Good work, Rafa. Tell the team they did a great job. We'll be back soon."

Ellie already had an idea of what must have happened, but she didn't dare believe it till she heard it direct from Hal. "What happened?"

"My team did the sting," he said. "I was right about Kramer— he was the one reporting to Nagle. He and a bunch of Nagle's guys showed up at the 'safe house' with explosives and guns. My guys caught them on tape talking about how Nagle sent them to kill us. My team took the tapes to the FBI. Kramer and Nagle were arrested, along with all of Nagle's gang. The judge refused them bail, so they're all going to rot in jail until their trials. Ellie, you're safe!"

Ellie's heart lifted and lifted, until she felt light as air. After all that stress and fear and danger, she could finally get back to her old life.

Better than her old life— her new life with Hal.

"Guess you're out of a job," she teased.

His tone was light but his expression was serious as he replied, "Nah, I don't think I'm ready to give it up. You've got yourself a bodyguard for life."

Her desire for him, which had been muffled before by exhaustion and stress, abruptly rose up within her, intense and irresistible. She couldn't fathom how she'd spent nights in his arms and had done nothing but sleep. He was standing only a few feet away from her, but that seemed an unbearable distance.

"Ellie…" Hal's voice dropped to a low rumble.

His eyes had gone dark with desire. She could feel the heat between them, palpable as if she was standing in front of an open fire. Her breath caught in her throat, her heart pounding, her palms tingling. She wanted to rush to him, but her own anticipation paralyzed her.

Hal swept her into his arms. She'd experienced his sheer strength many times before, but it was still startling. Thrilling. He lifted her as if she weighed nothing, raising her to bring her mouth level with his. She wrapped her arms around his muscular shoulders as they kissed.

She could lose herself in the heat of his mouth, the roughness of the stubble that seemed to grow back almost as soon as he shaved it off, the silken fineness of his hair.

She could feel the steely rod of his erection pressing insistently against her thighs. Ellie rubbed against it, teasing him and herself, enjoying the game of making him tense and groan. He pushed back, thrusting against her and wringing a cry from her own lips.

"Put me down," she gasped. "I want you inside me, now!"

Hal set her down, then steadied her with his huge hands curving around her waist. She was weak at the knees, dizzy with desire. Sweat prickled along her spine, and she couldn't seem to catch her breath. He too had come undone, even in that short span of time. He was panting, his hair disheveled, his cheeks flushed.

"I can't wait either," he muttered.

He fumbled in his jeans pocket for a condom while Ellie undid his belt. His pants had gotten so tight in front that she struggled to unbutton them. When she finally managed it, he groaned with relief.

"I thought my pants were going to rip," he said.

Ellie giggled. "I'm glad I'm a girl."

She closed her hand around his rock-hard shaft, sliding her fingers up and down, enjoying Hal's gasps. A glistening bead appeared at the head. Ellie bent and licked it, wringing a groan from deep within his chest. His head was thrown back, his eyes closed and long lashes fluttering against his cheeks, the condom dangling forgotten from his fingers.

The sight of him made her hot all over. Her clit was throbbing, making her squirm. She could feel herself getting wet and slick. The same insistence she'd felt earlier overcame her, and she could wait no longer.

She pulled her head away. "Come on, Hal!"

Hal jerked his head up and tore open the condom packet, then rolled the latex over his thick shaft. She waited for him to pull off her dress, but instead, he reached under it to tug off her panties. He dropped them to the floor, around her ankles, and she stepped out of them.

Her entire body was trembling with eagerness, her sheer need an ache in her chest. Hal again reached under her skirt and trailed one finger along the slickness of her inner lips. Ellie cried out helplessly, writhing against his hand, rubbing her throbbing clit against his firm touch. She was shuddering, halfway to a climax, and he'd barely even touched her.

Hal wrapped one arm tight around her back, holding her steady, while he rubbed between her legs. She buried her face in his chest, lost in the joy of his touch, letting him bring her to an irresistible climax. The orgasm rippled through her body, and her cry was muffled against his chest.

Ellie lifted her head, panting, the aftershocks still making her inner walls contract in delicious pulses. It had been good, but she wasn't done yet.

"Go on," she said, when she could speak. "I'm ready for more."

"Me too," said Hal. He was smiling, but his hazel eyes burned with intensity.

He was still fully dressed, with only his jeans unzipped. So was she, in her shoes and flower print dress. But he once again lifted her into his arms, raising her high.

"Lift your dress," he said.

Excited, she grabbed the hem and raised it. She'd never had sex while a man held her in his arms before. With no sign of a strain, Hal slowly lowered her, settling her down on to his steely shaft. It slid in easily, filling her to the utmost. She gasped with pleasure. So did Hal.

"That feels incredible," he said.

"*You're* incredible," she replied.

Her hands clenched around his arms as he began to thrust inside of her. She wanted to close her eyes and abandon herself to the delights of physical sensation. But she loved watching Hal too, his intent yet joyous expression, his long eyelashes fluttering, the flush spreading over his skin, the pulse at his throat.

His shaft slid against her clit at every thrust, sending waves of heat through her body. Unlike the first orgasm, the second one built more slowly, allowing her to savor every moment of its inexorable approach. She held Hal tight, loving the journey they were taking each other on.

Her orgasm crashed over her like a tidal wave, carrying her far away from everything but her love for Hal and the pleasure of the sensation. She lost herself, dissolving in a sea of bliss. She was only distantly aware of Hal coming too, of his deeper cry, of the warmth swelling within her.

When she returned, she found that he had slid down the wall. They lay sprawled together on the kitchen floor. Hal reached out and tenderly brushed a curl of wet hair out of her eyes.

"Love you," he said softly.

She laid her head against his, cheek to cheek. "Love you too."

That night, the phone rang again. Ellie jumped nearly a foot in the air. But a moment later, she realized that it wasn't Hal's, but the old-fashioned telephone mounted on the wall.

Hal picked it up. "Hello?"

He mouthed "my parents" to Ellie, then said, "Yes, I'm here. Who tipped you off? Oh. Um... really? Uh... how much did he see?"

Ellie, wildly curious, shoved Hal's own phone at him. He typed on the screen, *One of my wilder cousins was having a late night in the woods. He saw me come in. He didn't see you— his view was from the back. But he got a great view of my ass.*

She stifled a fit of hysterics at the expression on Hal's face as he visibly fished for a reason to have been naked in the snowy woods at midnight. "Uh... It's a long story."

To Ellie, he typed, *Can I tell them about you?*

"Of course you can. I can't wait to tell Ethan about you!"

Hal turned back to the phone and told them the entire story, emphasizing how brave and beautiful and all-over wonderful Ellie was. Every now and then he stopped to hold the phone away from his ear, which was how she got to hear comments like "I told you so," and "So the two of you are going to move back home to start a family, right?" and "I want grand-cubs!"

Hal put his hand over the receiver. "They want to come over and meet you. Are you up to being nagged about how soon you're going to get pregnant? The correct answer is 'immediately.'"

Ellie shook her head frantically. She might feel better, but she didn't feel up to pregnancy nagging.

"Not yet," Hal said into the receiver. "We'll come visit you soon, all right? *Soon.* In a week, how's that?"

He spoke for a little longer, then hung up and resignedly turned to Ellie. "Well— At least the food will be good."

"It's kind of nice to get back to normal problems like nagging families."

Hal smiled and pulled her into his arms. "You know... I never thought I'd say this, but it kind of is."

Ellie leaned against Hal's chest, utterly content. She wanted nothing more in the world than what she had: her life, her work, her friends, her family, and her bodyguard bear.

EPILOGUE
Ellie

"I call Eleanor McNeil to the witness stand," announced the prosecutor.

There was a flurry of murmurs. The judge banged his gavel. "Silence in the court!"

Ellie swallowed. It was the moment she'd awaited for so long. She'd looked forward to it— once it was done, she'd be safe— but her heart fluttered in her chest at the thought of finally doing it.

"I never did like public speaking," she murmured.

Hal's strong arms gave her one final squeeze before he released her. He bent to give her the lightest kiss on the cheek as he said in his softest growl, "You're the bravest person I've ever known. Put him away. I'll be with you the entire time."

Her brother Ethan, who had returned from whatever classified location he'd been fighting in and was sitting on her other side, whispered in her ear, "Kick his ass all the way into the electric chair."

Hal's love gave her strength and courage, as did Ethan's faith in her ass-kicking skills. So did the sight of the entire team of Protection, Inc., who had turned out to support her. All of them were there, from tatted-up Nick to the gold-chained Lucas. Rafa gave her an encouraging grin, but she was equally grateful for the chilling stare Shane had fixed on Nagle. Curvy Destiny looked deceptively harmless, while slim Fiona radiated a coolly professional air of 'anyone who tries to get to the witness goes through me first.' Catalina couldn't come— she volunteered for Paramedics Without Borders, and had been called away to Europe to help with an earthquake— but she'd filled Ellie's phone with encouraging text messages.

Ellie walked steadily to the witness stand and told her story. The prosecutor had advised her not to look at Nagle in case he intimidated her, but she didn't take the advice. Instead, she stared steadily at Nagle as he sat handcuffed in the dock, hatred in his eyes.

But he didn't scare her any more. All his men had already been convicted, along with Detective Kramer. Nagle's own trial was the last one. And if he tried anything, Hal would bite his head off. Literally. And that was only if Ethan or Hal's team didn't kill him first. Ellie wasn't alone, she was surrounded by people who loved her and would die to protect her.

When the time came, she raised her arm and pointed straight at Nagle. "That's him. That's the man I saw in the alley who ordered the murder."

Nagle gave the slightest twitch of his hand, as if he was about to make a fist. A low, hair-raising growl echoed through the courtroom.

"Silence!" said the judge. "Who was that?"

Nobody spoke. But Ellie knew who it was. And Nagle sat still as a statue for the rest of her testimony, not even daring to look her in the eyes.

His sleazy defense lawyer tried to claim that Ellie was a liar, but she could see that the jury believed her. When she finally got down from the stand, she felt triumphant. She settled back down beside Hal on the hard court benches, and he took her hand.

"You were fantastic," he whispered.

"So were you," she whispered back. "Loved the growl."

The judge banged his gavel. "Silence in the court!"

"Ladies and gentlemen of the jury, have you reached a verdict?" asked the judge.

The foreperson stood up. "We have, your honor. We find the defendant, Wallace Nagle, guilty of all charges."

The courtroom erupted in cheers. Hal bent Ellie over and kissed her. She relaxed in his arms, all tension gone. When they finally broke apart, she saw that even the judge was smiling, his gavel unused beside his hand. Then he cleared his throat. Silence fell.

"Wallace Nagle, you are hereby sentenced to life in jail, with no possibility of parole. Maximum security." The judge banged his gavel. "Also, the court would like to commend witness Eleanor McNeil for her extraordinary courage and honesty."

The guards dragged away the red-faced, spluttering Nagle to begin serving his life sentence.

Half of Hal's team crowded around to congratulate her, and the other half formed a protective barrier between her and the reporters who had started to descend. Ethan hugged Ellie and smacked her on the back, then went to join the group fending off the reporters.

"My team and your brother have it covered," Hal said, jerking his chin toward the swarming journalists. "Let's take off. We can celebrate with them later."

It warmed Ellie's heart to see how much more relaxed Hal seemed than when she'd first met him, and how he now not only trusted his team to do their jobs, but to take some of the weight off his back.

"Good idea," Ellie said. "Let's go."

They left the courthouse hand in hand.

As he drove her back to the apartment they shared, Hal rested his hand on her thigh, a comforting anchor. "Do you feel safe now?"

"It's a relief, of course," Ellie replied. "And Santa Martina is definitely safer now that Nagle's in jail for life. But no matter what, I know I'm safe so long as you're with me."

Hal's voice dropped to a protective rumble. "Always."

She reached up and ruffled his hair, enjoying its silky texture and the warmth of his skin. Enjoying his voice, his presence, his strength. His steadfast love.

Ellie had no more doubts, about him or about herself. Hal would stand by her side, and she'd stand by his.

Always.

A NOTE FROM ZOE CHANT

Thank you for buying my book! I hope you enjoyed it. The next three books in the Protection, Inc. series are out now. Number two is *Defender Dragon*, starring Lucas, number three is *Protector Panther*, starring Shane, and number four is *Warrior Wolf,* starring Nick.

If you enjoy *Protection, Inc,* I highly recommend Lia Silver's *Werewolf Marines* and Lauren Esker's *Shifter Agents*. All three series have hot romances, exciting action, brave heroines who stand up for their men, hunky heroes who protect their mates with their lives, and teams of shifters who are as close as families.

The cover of *Bodyguard Bear* was designed by Augusta Scarlett.

SPECIAL SNEAK PREVIEW

DEFENDER DRAGON

PROTECTION, INC.
2

A NOTE FROM ZOE CHANT

I hope you enjoy this sneak peek at Lucas and Journey's first meeting!

"May I offer you the traditional drink of the royal family of Brandusa?" Lucas asked.

"Yes, please," she said. "I love traditional things."

"I can see. You wear our gown and shoes beautifully." He turned to the bartender. "Two flutes of dragonfire."

"Oooh…" Journey breathed. "That sounds exciting."

The bartender reverently took the bottle from beneath the bar, and poured out two flutes. The orange-red liquor roiled in the glasses like liquid flame, seething and sending up wisps of smoke before it settled.

"What's it made of?" Journey asked.

"See if you can guess, after you try it." Lucas offered her a glass, then took his. "There is a toast in three parts. You drink after each one. Match your sips to mine, so you finish on the third."

Journey nodded eagerly, then inhaled the air over her glass. "It smells like… I know it, but I can't put my finger on it…"

"Like fire?" Lucas asked. "Like hot metal?"

"Yes! I've never had a drink that smells like that." She glanced into the glass, and Lucas was secretly amused to see her visibly wondering if it would taste revolting, then resolve to be polite no matter what.

"The toast," he reminded her, holding up his glass, and she raised hers to meet his. "We raise our glasses to the three treasures of the dragon. To honor."

"To honor," Journey echoed, and drank with him.

It was impossible to get used to the taste of dragonfire. The liquor tasted of fire, of peaches plucked on a summer day, of dreams and hopes and desire. It curled like flames over the tongue and slid down the throat like molten gold.

Lucas felt the fire of the liquor spread throughout his body. He had to alter his stance; he'd gotten so hard, his breeches were tight. Dragonfire wasn't an aphrodisiac, exactly; it wouldn't make you desire someone if you didn't already. If you drank it with friends or family, it brought on a pleasant nostalgia for all the good times you'd shared. But if you drank it with a lover, the evening was likely to conclude with a wild night of passion.

Journey's eyes widened as she swallowed. She took a deep breath, making her ivory breasts move within the corset. A very light sweat sprang up, giving her exposed skin a lovely glow. She looked Lucas boldly over from head to foot, her eyes lingering at the bulge in his breeches, then hastily jerked her gaze back to his face.

He raised his glass again. "To gold."

"To gold," Journey repeated, and they both drank again.

She licked a scarlet droplet from her lips. Lucas watched her tongue moisten her full lips, and imagined it flicking against his. Tasting and caressing its way down his body. Tracing the dragonmarks on his belly and chest. Then licking further down…

He forced his mind away from those images, and lifted his glass for the final toast. "To the open sky."

No dragon could have spoken the final toast with more longing than Journey as she repeated, "To the open sky."

They drained their glasses. The dragonfire burned its way down his throat, sending tendrils of heat coiling around his limbs. Its flavor lingered on his lips, and its perfume surrounded him.

"I can still taste it," whispered Journey.

She leaned in as she spoke, making him long to bend down and taste it on her lips. Lucas felt dizzy, as if he was floating in flames, and couldn't tell if it was the dragonfire or being so close to Journey. She was barely a handspan away from him. He could feel the heat of her body. It was maddening that he couldn't touch her.

Then he realized that there was a way that he could.

"Dance with me," he said, and offered her his hand.

ZOE CHANT
COMPLETE BOOK LIST

All books are available through Amazon.com. Check my website, zoechant.com, for my latest releases.

While series should ideally be read in order, all of my books are standalones with happily ever afters and no cliffhangers. This includes books within series.

Books in Series

Protection, Inc.
Book 1: *Bodyguard Bear*
Book 2: *Defender Dragon*
Book 3: *Protector Panther*
Book 4: *Warrior Wolf*

Bears of Pinerock County
Book 1: *Sheriff Bear*
Book 2: *Bad Boy Bear*
Book 3: *Alpha Rancher Bear*
Book 4: *Mountain Guardian Bear*

Cedar Hill Lions
Book 1: *Lawman Lion*
Book 2: *Guardian Lion*

Book 3: *Rancher Lion*
Book 4: *Second Chance Lion*

Enforcer Bears
Book 1: *Bear Cop*
Book 2: *Hunter Bear*
Book 3: *Wedding Bear*
Book 4: *Fighter Bear*

Fire & Rescue Shifters
Book 1: *Firefighter Dragon*
Book 2: *Firefighter Pegasus*
Book 3: *Firefighter Griffin*
Book 4: *Firefighter Sea Dragon*

Glacier Leopards
Book 1: *The Snow Leopard's Mate*
Book 2: *The Snow Leopard's Baby*
Book 3: *The Snow Leopard's Home*
Book 4: *The Snow Leopard's Heart*

Gray's Hollow Dragon Shifters
Book 1: *The Billionaire Dragon Shifter's Mate*
Book 2: *Beauty and the Billionaire Dragon Shifter*
Book 3: *The Billionaire Dragon Shifter's Christmas*
Book 4: *Choosing the Billionaire Dragon Shifters*
Book 5: *The Billionaire Dragon Shifter's Baby*
Book 6: *The Billionaire Dragon Shifter Meets His Match*

Hollywood Shifters
Book 1: *Hollywood Bear*
Book 2: *Hollywood Dragon*
Book 3: *Hollywood Tiger*
Book 4: *A Hollywood Shifters' Christmas*

Honey for the Billionbear
Book 1: *Honey for the Billionbear*

Book 2: *Guarding His Honey*
Book 3: *The Bear and His Honey*

Ranch Romeos
Book 1: *Bear West*
Book 2: *The Billionaire Wolf Needs a Wife*

Rowland Lions
Book 1: *Lion's Hunt*
Book 2: *Lion's Mate*

Shifter Kingdom
Book 1: *Royal Guard Lion*
Book 2: *Royal Guard Tiger*

Shifting Sands Resort
Book 1: *Tropical Tiger Spy*
Book 2: *Tropical Wounded Wolf*

Upson Downs
Book 1: *Target: Billionbear*
Book 2: *A Werewolf's Valentine*

NON-SERIES BOOKS

Bears

A Pair of Bears
Alpha Bear Detective
Bear Down
Bear Mechanic
Bear Watching
Bear With Me
Bearing Your Soul
Bearly There
Bought by the Billionbear

Country Star Bear
Dancing Bearfoot
Hero Bear
In the Billionbear's Den
Kodiak Moment
Private Eye Bear's Mate
The Bear Comes Home For Christmas
The Bear With No Name
The Bear's Christmas Bride
The Billionbear's Bride
The Easter Bunny's Bear
The Hawk and Her LumBEARjack

Big Cats

Alpha Lion
Joining the Jaguar
Loved by the Lion
Panther's Promise
Pursued by the Puma
Rescued by the Jaguar
Royal Guard Lion
The Billionaire Jaguar's Curvy Journalist
The Jaguar's Beach Bride
The Saber Tooth Tiger's Mate
Trusting the Tiger

Dragons

The Christmas Dragon's Mate
The Dragon Billionaire's Secret Mate
The Mountain Dragon's Curvy Mate

Eagles

Wild Flight

Griffins

The Griffin's Mate
Ranger Griffin

Wolves

Alpha on the Run
Healing Her Wolf
Undercover Alpha
Wolf Home

IF YOU LOVE ZOE CHANT, YOU'LL ALSO LOVE THESE BOOKS!

Laura's Wolf (Werewolf Marines # 1), by Lia Silver. Werewolf Marine Roy Farrell, scarred in body and mind, thinks he has no future. Curvy Laura Kaplan, running from danger and her own guilty secrets, is desperate to escape her past. Together, they have all that they need to heal. A full-length novel.

Prisoner (Werewolf Marines # 2), by Lia Silver. Werewolf Marine DJ Torres is a born rebel. Genetically engineered assassin Echo was created to be a weapon. When DJ is captured by the agency that made Echo, the two misfits find that they fit together perfectly. A full-length novel.

Partner (Werewolf Marines # 3), by Lia Silver. DJ and Echo's relationship grows stronger under fire... until they're confronted by a terrible choice. A full-length novel.

Mated to the Meerkat, by Lia Silver. Jasmine Jones, a curvy tabloid reporter, meets her match— in more ways than one— in notorious paparazzi and secret shifter Chance Marcotte. A romantic comedy novelette.

Handcuffed to the Bear (Shifter Agents # 1), by Lauren Esker. A bear-shifter ex-mercenary and a curvy lynx shifter searching for her best friend's killer are handcuffed together and hunted in the wilderness. A full-length novel.

Guard Wolf (Shifter Agents # 2), by Lauren Esker. Avery is a lone werewolf without a pack; Nicole is a social worker trying to put her life back together. When he shows up with a box of orphaned werewolf puppies, and danger in pursuit, can two lonely people find the family they've been missing in each other? A full-length novel.

Dragon's Luck (Shifter Agents # 3), by Lauren Esker. Gecko shifter and infiltration expert Jen Cho teams up with sexy dragon-shifter gambler "Lucky" Lucado to win a high-stakes poker game. Now they're trapped on a cruise ship full of mobsters, mysterious enemy agents, and evil dragons! A full-length novel.

Tiger in the Hot Zone (Shifter Agents # 4), by Lauren Esker. In her search for the truth about shifters, tell-all blogger Peri Moreland has been clashing with tiger shifter and SCB agent Noah Easton for years. Now she and Noah are on the run with an unstoppable assassin after them and a custom-made plague threatening the entire shifter world! A full-length novel.

Made in the USA
San Bernardino, CA
11 January 2019